HEARTS ON FIRE SERIES

Hearts Ablaze
Burning Love
Heart's Desire
Unexpected Flames

THE JACKSON TRILOGY

Fighting for Us

TAPHOUSE BLUES SERIES

Stay With Me
Don't Say Goodbye

For Leaona
You inspire me every single day.
You're a bright light in the darkest room.
I cherish our friendship.
Thank you.
I love you always.

xo

PROLOGUE

Staring at my reflection in the mirror, I run a brush through my long brown hair. My brown eyes are empty, red-rimmed, and puffy. Setting my brush on the vanity, I take a deep breath and apply makeup to the dark bruises marring my skin. As I dab some concealer on, I clench my eyes shut at the reminder of Graham's latest episode.

Seven years ago, I was just a college graduate with my entire future ahead of me. But that night I agreed to be his wife, my life changed. We got married three months later, and only a month after that he hit me for the first time. Shocked and devastated, I rushed to the bedroom to pack where he dropped to his knees, pleading with me to forgive him.

And like the coward I am, I took him back.

Every. Single. Time.

I fell in love with Graham in our junior-year business class. I wanted to open my own clothing store, and he wanted to start a real estate company. Tall at six foot two, his blond hair and deep green eyes drew me in. He treated me like gold, taking me out every weekend. I gave him all of me, virginity included, and he set it all up in flames.

I have no idea who I am anymore. The violence has only become worse, and I'm scared every time I see that look in his eyes. The pure hatred. I don't know what

I've done wrong. Now, instead of owning the business I always dreamed of, I'm stuck in our house, waiting on him hand and foot. Three years ago, Graham opened his own company with his best friend, and it took off like a bat out of hell. It's thriving, and he makes sure I know every day that every dime is his.

I have to force the memories away, my hands shaking on the granite vanity. Counting to ten, I take a couple of deep breaths, trying hard to gain control of my emotions. We're supposed to go to my mother's house tonight for dinner. She's all I have in this world, and I need to make sure there are no traces of Graham's earlier actions.

Usually he makes sure to hurt me in ways that don't show. Twisting my arms, pulling my hair, slaps—they don't leave marks as often. But he used his fists to take out his frustration this time, and unfortunately my face took a few of the main blows.

When I'm satisfied I look okay, I straighten my shoulders and march out of the bathroom. Grabbing my purse that I left lying on the bed, I sling it over my shoulder and head downstairs to where Graham is waiting, finding him pacing in the foyer. He looks up at me with anger all over his face.

"Take long enough? Let's get this fucking evening over with. I have a meeting tonight."

Trying to hide my emotions, I brush past him to slip my feet into the heels I left by the door last night. He likes me dressed in fancy clothes, shoes that hurt my feet. I always have to look the picture-perfect image of his wife.

By 'meeting,' I'm assuming he'll be meeting up with one of his many female companions. We've been married just over seven years, and he hasn't touched me sexually in four. Not that I'd want to even if he did.

"I'm sorry, Graham," I mutter, turning to face him.

"Just shut up, Sadie. I'm not in the mood to hear your shit."

Grabbing the car keys off the table, he goes to open the door behind me when his cell phone starts ringing. Answering it, he strides right out the front door, leaving me behind. For just a moment, I imagine myself not following him. Instead, I'm running far away, never looking back.

One day.

Pulling the front door closed behind me, I head down the walkway to where his Mercedes is parked. I only make it a handful of steps before he's turning back toward me.

"I'm dropping you off and going to meet Nick."

"But we're having dinner with Mom. She's looking forward to seeing us."

"Don't care."

Narrowing my eyes, I let out a huff. "Forget it. I'll drive myself," I say, turning to go back inside. Graham comes up behind me and unlocks the door for me, and then he's gone, climbing into his car in seconds.

"Asshole," I grumble, slamming the door shut behind me. Kicking off my heels, I rush upstairs to change into a pair of flats, then grab the keys to our BMW and head out. Climbing in, I crank the engine and back out of our driveway.

The short drive to my mom's is made quietly. I don't bother with music, my thoughts too loud in my head. For the first time in my almost twenty-nine years on this earth, I'm tired. Tired of the abuse. The depression. But mostly I'm done with not knowing who I am anymore.

Graham has taken every ounce of my old self and destroyed it. I need to get away from him, need to start over. And I'm fucking terrified. I have no idea what to do.

Pulling into my mom's driveway, I park next to her older model Ford and climb out, not bothering to lock my doors. Strolling up to the front door, I let myself in with my own key.

"Mom, I'm here." Dropping my purse on the couch, I go into the kitchen, finding it silent and empty. "Mom?" I take the narrow hallway toward her room, the door half closed. Pushing it open, I step into the room, my world changing forever.

Lying in the center of the bed, she looks like she's asleep. I gently try waking her up with a hand on her shoulder. When she doesn't move, I lay my hand flat on her chest, but before I can jostle her, I realize her chest isn't rising.

"Mom!" Frantically I shake her, my pulse racing. I run out to the living room, finding my cell phone in my purse. My finger's shake as I dial 911, tears spilling down my cheeks.

"911, what is your emergency?"

"My mom, she's not breathing. I don't know what

happened!" Stumbling back to the bedroom, I do as the operator tells me, performing CPR on the woman who gave me life, the only person in this world who loves me. My entire life.

I have no idea how long I try to save my mother before the sirens sound in the driveway. I don't stop until I'm being pulled off my mom, told to step aside so they can help her. I watch in horror as they do everything they can for her. Walking backward, I hit the wall and slide down it, teeth chattering as I cry. A police car pulls in, lights flashing wildly.

I'm broken from my daze by one of the paramedics crouching in front of me, their eyes sad. "I'm so sorry, but she's gone."

"No, you have to save her. Please."

"We tried everything, but she was already gone."

Shaking my head, I force myself to stand up, taking the few steps over to the bed. Bending over, I rest my head on her chest and cry, gripping one of her hands in mine.

"Please, you can't leave me, Mom. I need you too much. I love you, please."

Gentle hands pull me back and I fight against them, not wanting to let her go. The officer holding on to me guides me out to the living room, helping me sit on the couch. I'm asked questions I don't want to answer. I ask questions they can't answer.

My mother is gone. Nothing can make this okay.

Hours later, I arrive back home, eyes swollen and hurting, but not nearly as bad as my heart. Words like 'autopsy' and 'funeral arrangements' aren't ones I ever thoughts I'd hear.

The house is empty, Graham not home yet from his evening plans. Silently, I walk up the stairs to the bedroom, unable to feel or think. Stripping down to my underwear, I pull a tank on and climb into bed, pulling the blankets over my head. Burying my face in my pillow, I cry, soaking the pillowcase with my heartache.

I never heard Graham come home, unable to sleep all night. When the sun rises, I head into the bathroom, splashing my face with cold water. The bruises from yesterday stand out against my pale skin. Pulling on my robe, I head down to the kitchen to make some coffee.

I'm just taking the canister out of the cabinet when the sound of the front door opening breaks the silence. A moment later, Graham comes walking in the kitchen, still dressed in his clothes from the night before. He tosses his jacket onto the kitchen island and trains his eyes on me, disgust laced through his features.

"What the hell is your problem?"

"Nothing," I whisper, going about loading the coffeepot.

He maneuvers around me to grab the orange juice from the fridge.

"Why are there dirty dishes in here?" he asks, motioning toward the sink.

"I didn't have a chance to do them," I say, placing the coffee back in the cabinet.

"Didn't have a chance? What, while you were sitting

around on your lazy ass doing nothing?"

"No."

"Fucking clean this mess up, then. For God's sake, you're as useless as a fucking wet towel."

Tears brim in my eyes as I go over to the sink. They spill over when I see what he's so pissed off at—three glasses and a couple plates.

Quickly I get them clean, and I'm placing the final glass in the strainer when he painfully grabs my arm, spinning me around until he's in my face.

"Christ, what is it gonna take for you to get that I'm the one in charge here? You do what I say, when I say it. Got it, bitch?"

"Got it," I repeat, brushing away the tears on my cheeks.

"You disgust me."

Roughly shoving me back, he places his empty glass in the sink, and I force myself to say the words that cause me more pain than his hands just did.

"My mom died."

Looking over his shoulder, he trains his eyes on me. I somehow hope he'll show me sympathy. Maybe an ounce of love. The twenty-year-old Graham I fell in love with would have, but this man in front of me is a stranger. And his answer only wounds me further.

"So fucking what?"

My eyes close at his words, the pain searing through my heart. His footsteps echo through the house as he moves upstairs, leaving me alone with my grief.

Dropping to my knees in the middle of the kitchen floor, I sob loudly, never feeling more alone or broken.

My life will never be the same. And I have no idea how I'm going to continue on.

CHAPTER ONE

NACOLE

SIX MONTHS LATER

Slapping my palm on top of the alarm clock makes the shrill beeping die as I roll over, the sun streaming right into my face. Grumbling, I push myself up from the bed to a sitting position. Wiping the sleep from my eyes, I yawn and stumble to the bathroom, hurrying through my normal routine before heading back to my bedroom to get dressed.

As I'm pulling on a pair of jeans, I glance over at the clock—8:00 a.m. I have an interview today at this sports bar in Nashville. I never thought at almost thirty years old I'd be working as a waitress when I have a business degree. But here we are.

Satisfied with my simple outfit of a black sweater and jeans, I make my way to the kitchen for coffee. My interview isn't until ten, but I only have a couple street directions on a piece of paper. When I received the call the other day about coming in, I explained that I didn't have GPS on my cell phone and I was given the basic instructions. I only have a couple hundred dollars left over from what I came to Tennessee with.

Almost four months ago, I left Graham Ward. After losing Mom, I was completely lost in my grief. I wanted to have a service for her, but she was cremated, much to my devastation. He didn't even allow me to purchase an urn for her. I still have her in the cardboard box the funeral home gave me.

Two weeks after her death, I received a phone call from a lawyer I'd never heard of. My mom left everything to me and had given her lawyer a letter to give me. Inside, she told me that she had been putting money aside for years. It's for me to do with as I please, but Graham was to never know. She hoped that someday I could be rid of him.

She knew everything.

All those years I thought I was clever at hiding bruises, any injuries, but I should've known. Mom knew me better than anybody. She didn't have much, but between her life insurance and her savings, I had a large nest egg of about $100,000. While that's not a whole hell of a lot in San Diego, it's more than enough in a small Tennessee town.

Graham never let me have much of anything, but the one thing I did have for years was time. I spent all my time waiting on him hand and foot, and the one thing I loved more than anything was country music. I still do. It's soothing, and it heals my heart. When I started looking into leaving my husband, the first place I thought of was Nashville. Starting over was scary, and while I find myself looking over my shoulder at every noise, I know it was worth it.

Check from my mom's lawyer, Mr. Hale, in hand, I pull the large glass doors to the bank open and stroll inside, eyes darting around, sure Graham followed me. Making my way up to the teller, I inform her that I need to open an account with just my name on it.

Thirty minutes later, I leave the bank with a navy folder and an account with six figures—all of which my husband knows nothing about. My next move is to leave, and the sooner the better. My body can't take any more abuse, nor can my mind handle the pain another day. Losing Mom showed me just how big of a monster I'm married to.

Every night, he comes home wanting dinner to be ready. Then I'm to leave him alone for the remainder of the evening. If dinner is even a minute later than he wants, I have to be 'dealt with' somehow. Last night he almost broke my arm, he twisted it so far back. Luckily I had some painkillers left over from his last episode and the throbbing has dulled enough for me to function.

Climbing into the Mercedes, I toss the folder on the passenger seat and hang my head, tears burning my eyes. "I'm doing it, Momma. I promise. I'm gonna get away."

Wiping at my face, I start the car and pull out into traffic, heading toward the law office I found online. I can do this. I just need to hang on a little longer

I'm broken from my thoughts by my cell phone

ringing loudly on the counter. Glancing at the screen, I find my attorney's name flashing on it.

"Hello?" I answer, gripping the phone tightly.

"Mrs. Ward, Mitchell Hale here."

"Mr. Hale, yes. How are you?" I swallow down the bile at even the mere mention of my last name.

"I'm doing just fine. So listen, last we spoke, you still hadn't filed from your husband. We have the documentation of his abuse, so I wanted to see if you'd changed your mind."

"No. I'm not ready. I know I'm being stupid, but the repercussions of filing for divorce…."

"I understand, but with what we have against him, there would be no defense for him."

"Still. Once I'm ready to take him on, I will. Right now I need to rest my mind. Mom hasn't been gone that long, Mr. Hale."

"Please, call me Mitchell. You'll let me know when you're ready, yes?"

"Of course. I can never thank you enough for everything."

"You're welcome. You doing okay? You're safe?"

"Yes. Trying to move on. I have a job interview today, and then I can start finding a permanent home. This apartment is terrifying."

"Terrifying?"

"Yeah. It's this rickety old place, spiders everywhere, and I can hear my neighbors fighting at all hours of the night."

"You know you have—"

I cut him off, knowing exactly what he's gonna say. "I know Mom left me enough money to take care of a better place to live, but I don't want to touch it. I don't want her money. I want her." My voice breaks off and I fight through the still raw emotions. "I'll think about it."

"Honey, can I be frank with you?"

"Yeah."

"Your mother wanted you to have the money to start over. She saw you spend years of your life beaten down and unhappy. I know losing her hurt you, and to be honest, it hurt me too. She wasn't just someone who I helped legally. She was my friend. And I'm certain she'd hate to know the tools she left you weren't being used."

"I know."

"Just think about it, okay? I'll check on you in a couple weeks."

"Bye."

Ending the call, I blow out a breath and brush away the few tears that fell. Pushing off the chair, I stroll to the bathroom and check to make sure that the little makeup I put on isn't ruined. Glancing at the time, I see I need to leave for my interview. I was told it would only take about fifteen minutes to get there, but I want to make sure I'm not late.

Grabbing my purse, I sling it over my shoulder and head down to my car, my mom's used Honda. Glancing at the paper I wrote the directions on, I buckle up and take a deep breath.

Here goes nothing.

§

Twenty minutes later, I pull into the small parking lot of Walker's Taphouse. The drive was easy and I never missed a turn. Parking next to a large truck, I climb from my car and brush off my clothes, hoping I look good enough.

Locking the doors, I drop my keys into my purse and head inside. The main door is unlocked and I push it open, stepping inside to the bar. I imagine it looks different at night, but at the moment it's barely lit, only a few overhead lights on above the bar top.

Looking around, I don't see anyone.

"Hello?" I call out.

"We're closed!" a deep voice shouts.

"Oh no, I'm not here for a drink or anything. I'm Nacole Ward. I have an interview." My voice is quiet and I begin wringing my hands together, worried I'm too early.

Silence.

"I can… I can go." My nerves and anxiety get the best of me and I turn to leave, knowing this was a bad idea. I'm clearly not ready to be around people or work full-time yet.

As I move to the door, I hear loud footsteps and I brace myself.

"No, wait. Sorry. I'm sorry."

Turning back toward the voice, I find a man who

looks to be in his early thirties, light brown hair styled into some sort of fauxhawk, his deep brown eyes trained right on me.

"I'm Brody Walker, owner of the place. You're a little early, so I was trying to get some paperwork done beforehand. I didn't mean to be rude."

He holds his hand out to me and slowly I take it.

"That's okay. I can go hang out in my car until you're ready," I offer, folding my arms across my stomach.

"Oh God no. Come into my office. We can go ahead and start now."

With a kind smile, he holds an arm out to lead the way, and I hesitantly follow him into his office. I take a seat in the chair set up in front of his desk and cross my legs, palms sweaty. Brody drops into his own chair and leans his elbows on the desk, fingers toying with his shiny wedding band. My eyes follow his ministrations and he notices his actions.

"Sorry. I'm still getting used to it," he says, smile growing wider by the second.

"Oh?"

"Got married only a month ago. That's my wife, Lindsey." He points at a small photograph on his desk, a beautiful blonde smiling at the camera, Brody kissing her cheek in it.

"She's beautiful," I say, looking back at Brody.

"She is. I'm a lucky son of a bitch. Are you married?"

I don't even hesitate. "No, I'm not."

Lying. Great way to start an interview. But it's the only

way to protect myself.

"One day," he jokes, reaching over for a manila folder. Removing the application I filled out earlier in the week, he places it in front of him. "So, Nacole Ward, tell me about yourself."

"Not much to tell," I say, wringing my hands together again.

"Says here you're from California. Whereabouts?"

San Diego.

"Santa Barbara," I lie again. I doubt he'll go digging into my background, but I don't need to give him any reason to accidentally stumble upon Graham.

"Always wanted to go there."

"It's beautiful. You should."

Brody nods, scanning the sheet in front of him. "Duly noted. So, what brings you all the way to Nashville?"

His words have the past six months flashing through my brain. The last time Graham took his rage out on me. My mother. I barely notice the tears filling my eyes until I look up and see the concern in Brody's.

"A fresh start," I whisper. He offers me a box of tissues and I gratefully take it. "Sorry, it's just been a hard few months. I lost my mom unexpectedly back in January, and I just needed to get away. Start over."

Brody's eyes soften, and he gives me a sad smile. "I'm very sorry to hear that."

"Thank you."

With a nod, Brody steers the conversation back to the interview, and I'm grateful.

"I'll cut to the chase, Nacole. When you came in and filled out the application, my bartender, Nate, knew you would be a good fit. He has a way of reading people. You're the only person interested in the job, and I like you."

"Seriously?" *I just bawled all over his desk and he's telling me I have the job.*

"Seriously. I know it's listed as a full-time job, but you can set when you work. Weekends will be best for tips, and since this place is small, we only have one other waitress, Caroline. She's been here since the beginning and she's amazing. She'll make sure you're taken care of. Pay is ten an hour, plus tips. I know most places pay shit for waitressing, but I refuse to pay anyone below that. Maybe that's why it took a couple years for this place to take off."

"Thank you. Really, I appreciate this so much."

"You're welcome."

We both stand from our seats, and Brody reaches out to shake my hand. "Welcome to Nashville, Nacole. Looking forward to getting to know you."

With a smile, I offer him a soft "Thank you" and turn to leave. It's not until I'm safely in my car with the doors locked that I let my head fall to the steering wheel, tears coursing down my cheeks. Guilt and excitement take over my heart. I hate knowing I couldn't be fully truthful with Brody, but I can't chance Graham finding me. If he does, he'll make sure I'm back where he thinks I belong, by his crooked and abusive side.

But I relish this chance.

The chance to finally start over and find myself again.

To take my life back and live for me and only me.

Nobody will ever dictate what I do. Nobody will control my thoughts, my desires, or my happiness ever again.

CHAPTER TWO

GARRET

"You have the right to remain silent. Anything you say can and will be used against you…"

Cuffing the arrogant bastard in front of me, I walk him over to the squad car. As I finish reading him his rights, I cup his head and shove him into the back seat. Groaning, I turn to my partner, Jace, who is standing at the back of the suspect's car.

"You believe that shit?" he says, anger all over his face.

"Blew twice the legal limit and had the balls to say he hadn't been drinking."

"Could've killed someone." Jace shakes his head, then strolls over to the open door and slams it shut. As cops, we see insane shit every day, but someone driving drunk is still the one thing that gets both of our tempers flared. Stupidest fucking thing anyone could ever do.

Twenty minutes later, we're almost back to the station, Jace steering the car in silence. We're at the end of a long-ass shift, and all I can think about is getting home, taking a hot-as-hell shower and grabbing a greasy burger for dinner. Tomorrow is my day off, and I plan on taking advantage of it.

"Wanna grab a burger tonight?" I ask.

"Brody's?"

"Sure. Or we could hit that new diner on Sheffield."

"Whatever you want, man."

An hour later, I'm in the locker room changing into street clothes. Heading out, I fist-bump Jace and tell him to meet me at Walker's in an hour. He agrees and I walk out of the station, stopping at my desk on the way. Seeing I have no messages waiting for me, I head out to my Jeep, tossing my shit in the back seat.

Cranking the engine, I roar out of the parking lot, quickly eating up the two miles to my house. As I turn in the driveway, my phone vibrates in my pocket. Taking it out, I kill the engine and pull the keys from the ignition. Looking at my phone, I see a text from my brother.

Brody: Mom just called. BBQ at their place tomorrow. Noon.

Garret: Roger that. You at work tonight?

Brody: Nah, Nate's there. Taking my wife to dinner.

Garret: Say hi to Linds for me.

Brody: Will do, bro.

Locking my phone, I climb from my vehicle and grab my duffel, swinging up the front steps. Shutting the door behind me, I toss my stuff into the laundry room and head straight for my bathroom. Turning the shower on, I wait for the water to heat up as I stare at my reflection in the mirror. I know I should probably shave, but I don't feel like it. I just want to get going.

When the water's ready, I strip and climb in, the hot spray feeling amazing against my sore body. Twelve hours and we barely did anything. The arrest earlier was the only one we had; otherwise, it was mostly just a bunch of driving around and only a few calls. A surprisingly quiet Saturday shift, and I'm glad it's over.

Now it's time for more important things.
Like food.

§

"Garret!"

Coming around the side of my parents' house, my sister in-law Lindsey comes rushing over to me, throwing her arms around my neck to hug me tight. Chuckling, I squeeze her hard and pull away with a smile.

"Hey, Linds."

"You mind keeping those paws off my wife, asshole?" Brody greets, coming to loop his arms around Lindsey's shoulders, pressing a kiss to her head.

"Oh please. Not her fault she didn't get the hot Walker," I tease, reaching out to smack my little brother on the head. He laughs and we all walk over to the outdoor table and chairs my mom has set up.

"Garret, honey, there you are." Mom stands from the table to kiss me and I wrap my arms tight around her, smiling when she lets out an "Oof."

"Hey, Momma."

I'm thirty-three years old and my mom is still the only woman in my life. I love the hell out of her, and she knows we're all crazy about her. And boy, does she use that to her advantage.

We take our seats at the table, and she looks at me with a smile. "How's work?"

"Can't complain. Busy as always."

"How's Jace?" she asks, grabbing a pitcher filled with her homemade lemonade and pouring me a glass. I take it and chug half of it in a couple sips.

"He's good. He was gonna come with me, but Drew needed his help at the shop."

"Next time," she says, looking up when Dad walks outside.

"Garret, good to see you, son." He claps me on the shoulder and I nod.

"Hey, Dad."

He sets the platter in his hands loaded with burgers and hot dogs next to the grill and looks around. "Ready to eat?" he asks, firing up the grill a moment later.

"Hell yes," I reply, finishing my lemonade.

Lindsey laughs and I look over at her. "What?"

"Between you and Brody, I'm not sure how your parents didn't go broke trying to feed you. Brody was just eating a sandwich before we left to come here."

"Hey, I'm a growing boy, what can I say?" Brody laughs.

"Yeah, growing boy. It's a shame you never grew to your full height," I throw back.

"Fuck you, man."

"I'm good, but thanks."

"Oh, would you boys please grow up," Mom says, shaking her head at our bickering.

"If we haven't by now, we never will," I tell her with a wink.

Brody starts cracking up, and Mom shakes her head with a smile.

Leaning back in my chair, I look up to see my dad disappear into the house, returning a minute later with beers. He hands one to me, and I take it and twist the top off.

"So, I kind of have some news," I announce, and Mom looks at me with a huge grin.

"You met someone?"

I choke out a laugh. "Uh, no. No I did not, Mom."

"Hell hasn't frozen over, so that's not possible," Brody chimes in.

"I've decided to take the detective's exam in a couple of months," I share.

"Oh, Garret, I think that's a wonderful idea, honey."

"Thanks, Momma."

"Fuck yeah, bro." Brody stands up and comes around the table. I stand as well and he gives me a fast hug, smacking me hard on the back.

"Thanks, man."

"You and Jace have been riding together for ten years now. How does he feel about it?" Brody asks.

Taking a pull from my beer, I set it down in front of me. "You know how he is. He loves being a cop. I think he wants to move up, but he just really loves what he's doing. Jace isn't ready, but I am. We talked about it last night when we went to get dinner, and I have his support 100 percent."

"Glad to hear it," Dad says, lifting the lid to start loading the grill.

"Need any help?" I ask. When he nods, I stand up and move over to him, holding out a hand for the platter of food.

It's not much longer before we're all digging into the food and chattering about random things, enjoying the meal but mostly the company.

§

A week later, I find myself sharing a table at my brother's bar with Jace and Lindsey, Brody tending the bar. It's a Friday night, so the place is crawling with people.

Reaching for the pitcher of Bud in the center of the table, I pour myself another beer and lean back. I gotta hand it to my little brother. When he opened this place years ago, we were all worried he'd drown under the pressure in a city like Nashville. But he's done damn good for himself, and I couldn't be prouder of the guy.

"How's the hospital, Linds?" Jace asks, taking a sip of his water.

"It's good. Been working a ton of overtime, which is great for the bank but bad for my personal life. I'm exhausted, but they just hired three new nurses, so it should be slowing down soon."

"That's good. How's Hollie doing?" I ask.

"Hollie is Hollie. Still too loud and obnoxious, still the best friend I've ever had." Lindsey laughs and takes a sip of her wine. She opens her mouth to say something else, but a crash behind us has me turning around.

A young woman is on her hands and knees, trying to clean up a spilled beer, shattered glass everywhere. Lindsey hops up from the table and rushes over to help, giving the woman a smile.

Turning back to Jace, I find Brody walking over, a tense look on his face. "She okay?" he asks, wiping his hands on a rag.

"Who, Lindsey?"

He shakes his head. "No, Nacole. My new waitress." He points to the woman Lindsey is helping. It's only then that I notice the gray Walker's T-shirt on her tiny frame.

She stands up a second later, brushing off her black shorts. I can't see her face, but her dark brown hair is in some sort of bun on top of her head, strands falling in her face. When she raises her head, I see dark brown eyes and a full mouth.

I don't even realize I'm staring at her until Brody

clears his throat.

"Sorry, what?"

Brody laughs at me, and Jace shakes his head.

"Earth to Garret."

"Who is she?" I ask, not even bothering to hide my interest.

"Nacole Ward. I hired her last week. She just moved here from Santa Barbara."

"Uh-huh." I'm not even paying attention. Her name was the only thing that registered out of my brother's mouth, my attention back on her. She's shorter than Lindsey, with curves in all the right places. When she gives Lindsey a small smile, her teeth are white and straight. She bends over to pick up the tray she was using, granting me full view of her ass, and I groan, my dick coming to life in my pants.

"Garret, for fuck's sake, man. Did you even hear what I said?" Brody waves in my face, laughing when I still don't turn around. I'm too captivated by this brunette beauty in front of me. I have no idea what it is about her, but I'm completely drawn to her.

I'm caught a minute later when Nacole's eyes catch mine, and I wink at her. Her cheeks darken and she turns on her heel, rushing back to the kitchen. Shaking my head, I turn back to my brother and Jace, rolling my eyes when they both start laughing at me.

"Damn, man. You didn't even say a word and she ran from you. That's a new record." Jace slaps me on the shoulder and I shrug him off.

"Aw, it's okay, bro. Maybe you can work your Walker charm and get a date out of her," Brody suggests, walking back over to the bar to help a new patron.

Lindsey comes back over to the table a few minutes later, completely unaware of my newfound interest in Nacole. But I find myself looking over Nacole's way every chance I get. I want to know her story, and one way or another, I'm gonna find out what it is.

Hours later, we're leaving the bar and heading out to Jace's truck when I bump into someone. Looking to my side, I see Nacole standing there, a to-go bag in her hand.

"Sorry," she whispers, rushing ahead of us and out of the bar, climbing into an old Honda and she pulls out a second later. I watch her taillights take her down the main drag out of town, and I can't help wondering why she was in such a hurry.

I like a good mystery. And Nacole Ward is certainly the one I want to figure out.

CHAPTER THREE

NACOLE

My first week at Walker's is over, and man, am I beat. That place is absolutely insane on weekends, and yet somehow I've never been happier. I made a decent amount of money in tips, and Caroline, the girl who's been training me, is an absolute sweetheart. Super bubbly and warm, she made me feel welcome right away.

Brody's wife, Lindsey, is incredible. When I knocked the beer off the table tonight, she didn't even blink an eye or get angry with me. After rushing over to help me clean it up, she gave me a few pointers and I thanked her profusely. But even in the rush of the evening, I didn't miss the blue-eyed man at her table all night.

I swear, I felt his eyes on me before I even noticed him. And when I locked gazes with those eyes, I could sense his intensity even across the bar. And that wink? Dead. I was completely dead.

Not that it matters. I'm not here to make friends or

play house with anyone, no matter how attractive they are. I'm here to start a new life.

To stay safe, no matter how long I need to be here.

And then stupid me had to go running into him on my way out, a late-night dinner from the kitchen in my hands. I mumbled an apology and rushed past him, noting how good his cologne smelled and how hard the chest I'd bumped into was. *Shit.*

Forcing all thoughts of the man from my head, I close the flimsy door to my apartment behind me, turning the only lock and hitting the light switch with my elbow. Dropping the plastic bag on the counter, I kick my sneakers off and stride into the bedroom, quickly changing into a pair of pajamas. Heading back to my dinner, I grab the Styrofoam container and carry it over to my couch, the only piece of furniture in my living room besides a coffee table.

I'd sort of hoped when I found the ad for a furnished apartment that it would have a bit more, and I make a mental note to buy a cheap television tomorrow. I didn't want to buy things I wouldn't need right away, not knowing how long it would take me to find a job, but now that I'm feeling settled, I could use some entertainment on my days off.

Mitchell's words from last week haunt my thoughts, and with a mouthful of chicken, I reach for my cell phone, pulling up a local realtor's site. My internet is shitty at best, so it takes me forever to find a number. When I do, I save it in my phone to call tomorrow. Can't hurt to see if there's a nice place in town I can look in to.

What's the worst that can happen?

§

"Nacole? Hello, I'm Stanley Harmon. So nice to meet you."

The middle-aged man comes around the desk in front of me, holding his hand out to shake. Stanley is the realtor I spoke to this morning, and he already has a few showings set up.

"Hi," I reply, genuinely excited. I did a lot of thinking last night and Mitchell is right. Leaving Graham was the first step; now I need to not continue living in shit. Mom may not have been ready to leave me, but she made sure I was okay.

No more hiding from myself.

"So I found a couple places to go check out, all well within your budget. One of them is a serious fixer-upper, much larger than the other, but it's on a smaller lot on the outside of town. The other is in much better shape with a small yard, but it's only around six hundred square feet."

Nodding, I follow him over to the front door. He holds it open for me and motions to his car, offering to drive us to both properties. I accept his offer and climb into the vehicle, my hands sweaty and nerves on edge. Getting into the car with a stranger is something I'm terrified of, but I'm trying my best to keep it together.

Arriving at the first property a few minutes later, I'm

immediately in love. Clearly this is the smaller of the two, but I don't care. It's on a more secluded lot, and it's perfect. Getting out of the car, I walk around the back of the house and find a small deck with a few potted plants, the lawn well kept.

Unlocking the door, Stanley ushers me inside where I'm met with a small eat-in kitchen. It reminds me so much of my own mother's house that it takes everything I have to keep it together. Pushing all the memories away, I take a walk through the rest of the house, finding a large master suite at one end, the living room on the other. It's all so homey and well taken care of that I'm sold.

Heading back to the kitchen where Stanley's waiting, I paste on a large smile.

"I'll take it," I announce, and he beams at me.

"Fantastic. Now you had mentioned paying cash? This place is eighty thousand, but if you wanted to try and put in a lower offer, I think you would find the seller willing to negotiate."

"No, eighty is fine. I was left money when my mother passed, and I'm planning on using it to find a home. And I think I found it." Running my hand over the blue granite countertops, I smile, imagining this place as my own.

"Well, welcome home, Nacole. Let's head over to the office and draw up the paperwork. If all goes well, then this time next week you'll be able to move in."

"Sounds good." Taking one last look around the house, I follow him back to his car.

As we drive back to the office, I fight tears, picturing

my mom. I miss her so much. I feel so guilty that I didn't get away from my husband sooner. I could've left and taken her with me.

So much time lost. And I'll never get it back.

§

"Over on Birch Road? Yeah, I know that area. You did well, girl." Lindsey stands on the other side of the bar, filling my table's drink order. I was telling her about my new place when I first got in, but we didn't have much time to chat.

"Yeah. Now I just need to find time to move the little furniture I have. I found a secondhand shop downtown and ordered a few much-needed things, but they're all gonna have to be picked up and moved too. Shit, I didn't think this through."

Lindsey raises an eyebrow at me, her eyes lighting up. "Brody can help! His truck should be able to hold everything, and I'm sure he can get Garret to help him too."

"Garret?" I ask, taking the tray from her, three beers all ready to go.

"Yeah, his older brother. Let me shoot him a quick text, and then we can set up a time that works for everyone."

"Thank you, Lindsey. I appreciate that."

"Anytime."

After carrying the drinks over to my table, I can't help smiling at Lindsey's kindness as I bring the tray back to the bar.

§

Later that night, I'm finishing up at a rowdy table when my cell phone vibrates in my back pocket. Rushing out back toward the bathrooms, I see it's Mitchell calling, so I answer.

"Hello?"

"Hey, glad I caught you."

"Everything okay?" I ask, trying to keep my voice down.

"Yeah, I just wanted to see how you're doing."

The tone of his voice spooks me, and I turn my back to the bar, stepping farther down the hallway. "What? What is it?"

"I saw Graham."

My heart races. I feel close to vomiting. "What?"

"I was out to dinner with a colleague, and I saw him enter the restaurant with another woman. Petite and blonde."

I blow out a breath. "Yeah, that's one of the usual girls."

"I think it's time. Clearly he's not waiting for you to come home."

"I'll think about it."

"Can I be honest with you, Sadie?"

Tapping my foot to a beat, I pace in a small circle. I wish he'd stop using my first name, the sound of it stirring up unwanted, painful memories. I sigh, knowing exactly what's coming. "Of course."

"He's an arrogant, abusive son of a bitch. He doesn't give one damn about where you are, what you're doing. I see too many of these kinds of cases, and I don't want to see you hurt. Again. Okay?"

"Okay."

"You're a brave woman, and your mother would be so proud of you. But now you need to put this all behind you. You'll never be able to move on until you do. Just don't lose hope."

"How can I lose what I've never had? Thank you, but I need to get back. I'm moving in just a couple days, so I'll call you once I'm settled."

"Finally letting her take care of you, huh?" I can hear the sadness in his tone.

"I owe it to her," I whisper, and with that I end the call, tucking my phone back into my pocket. With a deep breath, I head back out to the floor, pushing all thoughts of my mother and Graham aside.

With it closing in on eleven, my shift is just about over. I look toward the front door when I hear it open and see a group of guys come strolling in, heading for one of my tables. I groan, knowing I'm gonna be stuck here later than when my shift ends, but then Lindsey comes strolling over, bumping her hip into mine.

"Why don't you take off early? I got these idiots. Some of the guys from the firehouse downtown."

I give her a grateful smile. "Thanks. Did you ever talk

to Brody?"

"I did. We'll meet you at the furniture store Saturday so we can load everything from there and go. Does ten work for you?"

"Sounds perfect."

Lindsey tells me to have a good night, and I head out back to grab my stuff. Shoving my apron into my purse, I swing out the door to my car, a genuine smile on my face. Climbing into the driver's seat, I start the engine and look up to a butterfly on my windshield. It feels so out of place, but it brings me a sense of peace.

I love you too, Mom.

§

Saturday arrives with sun shining and a nice breeze coming through the open window. Pushing up to a sitting position, I stretch my arms and yawn, so glad to be leaving this dump. I hardly got any sleep last night, listening to the people above me screaming and yelling half the night, and then their music started blaring through the thin walls.

Getting out of bed, I head for the kitchen to make some coffee. It's only seven, so I have a little time before I need to be ready to go. Because the place came furnished—or their idea of furnished, anyway—I only have a few small boxes filled with personal belongings, so it won't take long.

Once my coffee is ready, I fill it with my favorite

flavored creamer and lean my hip against the counter. Lindsey texts, letting me know she's excited for today, and it dawns on me that while I've lived in this place for three months, I haven't done anything since I got here.

I spent the first two months grieving and barely leaving my bed. Lost twenty pounds and survived on a diet of coffee and peanut butter sandwiches. Since starting at Walker's a couple weeks ago, I've begun to gain some of the weight back.

I smile a bit wider.

I'm happy.

Finishing my coffee, I take a quick shower and forgo drying my hair, letting it fall down my back in wet strands as it air-dries. Dressing in a comfortable pair of jean shorts and a loose tank, I start packing what few items I have left.

An hour later, I'm sitting on the couch, looking around the house. Closing my eyes, I lean back against the couch and tilt my chin up.

I love you.

She's gone, but I know she can hear me.

§

"Hey, girl, you ready to get started?"

I'm at the furniture store, going through the list of items with the owner, when Lindsey and Brody walk in hand in hand.

"As I'll ever be. Thank you for helping today."

"No problem. Garret pulled in right behind us. Everything ready to go?" Brody asks, shoving his hands into his front pockets.

I nod just as the door opens again. I look over his shoulder, my jaw dropping in shock when the guy from last week comes strolling in, those blue eyes filled with amusement. He walks right over to me and holds out his hand.

"Hey, I'm Garret Walker. Nice to meet you, darlin.'"

Well fuck.

CHAPTER FOUR

GARRET

"Nice to meet you. I'm Nacole." Her soft voice fills my ears and I smile, gently shaking her hand. Brody asked me the other day if I would mind helping them move her into her new place, and I immediately agreed— anything to finally get to meet this beauty in front of me.

Nacole doesn't have on a stitch of makeup, and her eyes have a slight rim of pink around them, almost as if she'd been crying. That idea bothers me. This woman should never have any reason to be upset.

Whoa. Slow down, Walker. You don't even know her.

"Ready to get going?" I ask, and she nods, tucking a loose strand of hair behind her ear.

Turning back to the counter, she grabs the sheet of paper and points to the front of the store. "All of those are mine. I don't know what will fit, so we may have to take two trips."

A large worn sofa, along with a coffee table, a few lamps, and various other pieces sit marked by the front window. Pretty sure it'll all fit in Brody's truck in one go without a problem.

"Do we need to get your bed from the apartment?" Lindsey asks.

Nacole shakes her head. "No, I ordered it from a store at the mall. They delivered it last night, so it's already there. I didn't get too much stuff, just enough to start making the place mine."

Lindsey claps her hands together and we all start moving everything out to Brody's truck. He and I each grab an end of the couch and haul it out. It doesn't take too long to get everything loaded up, and then Brody closes the tailgate.

"So, you guys can just follow me over, I guess?"

"Absolutely," I say, heading for my Jeep.

As we wait for Nacole to lead the way, I can't stop thinking about her. I've spent all of thirty minutes with her, but I like her already. She doesn't talk very much, but she's very aware. I caught her looking at me almost the entire time, and every time I smiled or winked, she blushed to the roots of her hair. I definitely have an effect on her too.

So lost in my thoughts, I barely notice that everyone is starting to leave. Throwing my Jeep in gear, I take off behind them, rolling my windows down as I go. It's a nice enough day that I wish I'd remembered to put the top down on it. The sun is shining and the breeze is incredible.

The drive to Nacole's place only takes fifteen minutes, and soon we're all turning into her driveway. A tiny ranch hidden by some overgrown bushes, it's not quite what I had pictured.

Parking my Jeep next to Brody's truck, I hop down and stride over to her.

"So this is the place, huh?" I say, stuffing my hands into my pockets.

"Yeah. It needs a little work, but I really like it."

"Will you show me?" I ask, giving her a warm smile.

"Yeah, okay." I follow her up the short walkway and wait for her to unlock the door. Pushing it open, I step inside and find us in a small living room, but not as small as I would've thought. She takes me through the house, and I watch her eyes light up when we hit the kitchen.

The small window over the sink has a view into the backyard, and it's actually cozy inside. It's small, but surprisingly it doesn't feel that way. Maybe it's the open floor plan, or maybe it's just the light that Nacole brings into each room. She's beautiful.

"I like it," I tell her, my smile widening when she rewards me with a large one of her own. "It definitely has potential. It's homier than my place, that's for sure."

"Really?"

"Yeah. Years ago, Brody and I were left plots of land by our late uncle, way out on the outskirts of town. Brody's was already cleared, but mine still had trees as far as you could see. I cleared the lot for a house and moved in a couple years ago, but it's pretty empty. I need to paint, and my mom has been itching to get her hands on the decorating, but with work I hardly have the time."

Nacole leans her back against the kitchen counter. "What do you do?"

"I'm a cop."

"That sounds… exciting?"

Laughing, I step closer to her. "Yeah, it can be. Most of the time, it's idiots drinking and driving, or kids playing music too loud. Occasionally we get a call because some tourist is trying to find their way into some musician's property. The usual."

She laughs and the sound is music to my ears.

"So, Brody said you moved here from Santa Barbara. What brings a Cali girl like yourself down here to the city of good ole country music?"

I don't miss the tears that fill her eyes before she turns away from me. With a slight shake of her head, she turns back to me. "A fresh start, I guess. I wanted to start over."

"I can understand that."

We're interrupted by a knock on the front door. Brody steps inside a second later with a smirk. "You kids decent, or can we come in?"

"Shut the fuck up, jackass," I grumble. Striding outside, I avoid eye contact with my stupid brother and pull the tailgate down.

"Just yanking your chain, bro."

"Yank your own chain, Brody."

Climbing up into the truck, I start moving stuff down so he can grab it. After carrying the coffee table inside, he comes jogging out a second later.

"Nah. You guys were in there awhile. You talk about

48

anything special?"

"No, just work and such. And even then she barely talked."

"Yeah." Brody scrubs a hand down his face and reaches out for the couch. "She's quiet. Didn't say too much to me when I interviewed her, but I could tell she was good people. Just needed a chance to get her feet on the ground. And she's turned out to be a great hire. Lindsey really likes her."

"She's not the only one," I mumble, and I don't miss the knowing look Brody throws my way.

Grabbing the other end of the couch, I start walking it off the truck and lean the end against the tailgate so I can hop down. Picking it up together, we carry it inside the house, Lindsey's and Nacole's voices coming from the bedroom.

"Nacole, where do you want this?" Brody yells, and she pokes her head into the room.

"In front of the window is great."

Nodding, we slide it under the window, then head out for the remaining lamp and end table. Brody takes the lamp into the living room while I carry the end table into the bedroom. Setting it by the side of the bed, I hear Brody curse from the living room.

"What's up, man?"

"Fucking hell. Beer vendor is at the bar, and according to Nate, the entire order is fucked up. Linds? We gotta go to the bar and get this figured out."

Lindsey looks at Nacole with a sad smile, but Nacole

just shakes her head. "Go ahead, it's okay. I need to make a trip to get groceries and some other stuff. Thank you for the help today though. Means the world."

Lindsey reaches out and hugs Nacole, who seems surprised and only pats her on the back.

Huh. Weird. She just seemed to clam up right before our eyes.

Brody and Linds say their goodbyes and head out, leaving me alone with Nacole in her bedroom. She was clearly in the middle of unpacking a few boxes sitting on her bed, and I'm unsure of what to do. I want to stay and spend more time with her, but I also don't want to make her uncomfortable. She's so timid and shy with me; I don't want to scare her or push her away before I even get a chance to make friends with her.

"I'm gonna get going too. Unless you need any help unpacking or anything."

"No, thank you, Garret. I really don't have much, but I appreciate the offer."

"Of course."

Standing on opposite sides of the room, we just look at each other, her brown eyes dancing around, avoiding any direct contact with mine. Nodding, I hold a hand up in a wave and smile at her.

"It was great meeting you. I'll see you around, okay?"

"Okay. Thank you for today."

"Anytime, Nacole."

Turning, I walk out of the room and make my way out of the house. I'm climbing into my Jeep when I see the flowers I brought. *Shit. Would probably help if I gave her the welcome present.* Grabbing them, I head back toward her house and knock quietly on the front door, but she doesn't answer. *Weird.*

Pushing the door open, I decide to just leave them in her kitchen, but I'm stopped in my tracks when I'm setting them down. Carefully, I walk down the short hallway and poke my head around the corner into her bedroom. Sitting in the center of the bed, knees drawn to her chest, she has her face buried in her arms, body shaking with broken sobs.

"Nacole?"

Her head lifts at the sound of my voice and she brushes tears off her cheeks, her eyes red and swollen. Trying to compose herself, she moves to the edge of the bed.

"Sorry, I thought you left."

"Yeah, I did, but I forgot the flowers I brought you as a welcoming present. They're in the kitchen. Are you okay?" Stupid question, but I don't really know what to do. Crying women aren't exactly my forte, and it usually brings me to my knees.

"Yeah, I'm fine. Sorry, just a little overwhelmed is all."

"You're sure?" I keep my voice gentle, running a hand through my hair.

She nods and puts on a brave smile, but I don't miss the tremble in her bottom lip.

"Okay. Can I get you anything before I leave?"

"Uh… no. No, I don't think so."

With a nod, I turn to leave once more, but the sound of her sniffling has me turning back to her with a sigh.

"Nacole?"

"Yeah?"

"There's something else I wanted to give you."

Wiping her eyes with the back of her hand, she stands up, and I close the space between us in just a couple strides. Placing my hands on her shoulders, I look at her puffy eyes and give her a small smile. Moving slowly so I don't freak her out, I pull her against my chest, hugging her carefully. She only hesitates for a second, and then her arms are banding around my waist as she buries her face in my chest. Keeping her tight to me, I rock her back and forth, whispering soothing words to her.

My shirt is soaked from her tears as her small frame trembles in my arms. Smoothing a hand up and down her back, I just hang on tight, letting her cry. Gently, I cup her head against my chest, placing a soft kiss against her hair, lips lingering while I cradle her to me.

I have no idea what's upset her so much, but I'm not sorry that she's in my arms. I'm a selfish bastard, but holding her feels right. Nacole fits against me perfectly, and I vow to myself that if she's ever in my arms again, no tears will be falling from her beautiful eyes.

§

"No, I swear. I've never been."

We're sharing a plate of French fries at a local diner,

a chocolate milkshake in front of each of us. After she calmed down earlier, I offered to take her out and get her mind off whatever had upset her.

"How have you never been to a country music concert? This is Tennessee, woman."

"I just moved here. It's not exactly on my to-do list."

"Well, I'm changing that."

"Garret…."

"I'm serious," I state, crossing my arms over my chest.

She sighs and fiddles with her straw before taking a sip of her milkshake. After a beat, she trains her eyes on me.

"Listen, I really appreciate everything you've done. Brody and Lindsey too. But I'm not at a place right now where I'm looking for friends. I know I'm being a total bitch, but I have to be honest."

"Hey, you aren't a bitch. Don't talk about yourself that way, all right?"

"Garret—"

"No, I'm serious. Clearly you're dealing with something. I'm not blind. And I'm not gonna push you into talking to me or forcing your hand, but please don't insult yourself for being honest, okay?"

Nacole's eyes widen briefly, but after a second she nods. "Okay."

"Now, you may not be looking for friends, and I can't speak for the others, but I'm always up for a new friend. You can never have too many of them."

"I don't have any," she says quietly with a shrug.

"Well now you have one."

Nacole smiles and nods at me. "Fine. We're friends," she concedes, then, in a surprising move, throws a french fry at my forehead, giggling when I throw it back at her.

"Now, back to the real issue," I begin, leaning my elbows onto the table.

"Issue?"

"Yeah. It's decided. I'm taking you to your first country concert. And I know just who to bring you to see. He's playing at a festival next month."

"We'll see," she says, but a small smile plays at her lips. She's already sold.

CHAPTER FIVE

NACOLE

"Graham, please. She was my mom," I sob, clutching at the sweater I'm wearing, desperate to get his approval.

"Exactly. Your *mom, not mine. That bitch hated me, so why should I do anything nice for her?*" He's annoyed, pacing in circles in front of me, and I know nothing I say will change his mind.

"I'm your wife. Do it for me, Graham. Please don't make me do this."

"Who gives a fuck what you are to me? I'm not wasting a dime of my money to bury her. They can dump her off the side of a cliff for all I care. Now stop this nonsense. I have work to do."

His words cut like knives, each blow more painful than the first. But I can't let him do this, I just can't. I need my mother to be taken care of.

Rushing after him, I grasp at his arms, fighting him to

stay, to talk, to have just a tiny piece of humanity. I don't see his hand before it's on my face, backhanding me with a strength I've never felt.

"Shut. Up. Sadie. For fuck's sake, look how pathetic you are. I have work to do, and I swear to God, if you don't stop fucking pestering me with this bullshit, I will give you something to cry about. Now enough!*"*

The skin he slapped burns under my hand. Tears fall down my cheeks as I manage to pluck up the only small piece of courage I have.

"Fuck you, Graham Ward. I hate you so much!"

I know I screwed up when he turns toward me, a menacing grin on his face. In three strides, he's right in front of me, his hand forcefully coming around my throat and squeezing. He backs me up and slams me against the wall, hand closing off my airway even more.

Gasping for air, I claw at him, but he's too strong.

"You hate me? Oh, sweetheart, you have no idea what hate is. Now I'm gonna tune you in to a little secret, okay." His face is inches from mine, and I smell the vodka he had with dinner on his warm breath. "While you were busy refusing to get out of bed and throwing fits, I took the call from the funeral home. Told them you'd decided to have her cremated, that you were unfit to make the call. Played the role as doting husband, and they ate that shit right up."

Tears pour down my cheeks as his hand tightens impossibly harder. He's inches from my face, grinning wildly at me. "So it's done, lovely wife. She's in a cardboard box waiting for you to pick her up. Or she can stay down there in a drawer where she belongs. Got it, sweetheart? Don't you ever think for one second that you're in control here, got it?"

I don't move, blackness starting to creep in on me.

"I said got it?" he growls, squeezing so hard my eyes bulge under his grip.

I nod as much as I can and he releases me, smiling while I struggle to take in a deep breath, coughing and holding my sore throat.

"Good. Now stay out of my sight. You sicken me."

He's gone a moment later, and I fall to the ground, back against the same wall he just had me pinned to moments before. Crying softly, I know the pain in my throat is nothing compared to the pain in my heart.

How could he do this?

Jerking awake from the nightmare I sit up in bed, heart pounding and tears pouring down my cheeks. Chest heaving, I stumble to my kitchen and pour myself a glass of water with shaking hands before sucking it down, trying desperately to calm down. Setting the glass on the counter, I glance at the time and see it's three in the morning.

Opening the back door, I step out onto the tiny porch and descend the stairs, going into my backyard. Standing in the quiet night, the breeze flinging my hair around, I take a deep breath and blow it out, counting to ten. My heart rate slows and I feel myself calming down as I fill my mind with images of my mom. Of her memory. Her smile.

Losing her was the worst thing I've ever been through, and I know it won't stop hurting overnight, but I need to push myself to try harder. Stop closing people out and start living. The more time I spend here in Tennessee, the more I immerse myself in relationships and my job, the more I want to live. Not just for Mom's memory, but for myself. I deserve that much.

Graham destroyed Sadie Nacole Ward. Broke her soul and turned her into a shell of who she used to be.

But Nacole Ward can be different. She can be strong. I just have to remind myself of that.

Deep down I know I should let my true self through, that they'd accept me for who I am, past and all. But until I'm finally free from Graham, I can never tell them who I really am.

Because telling them would mean I'd have to be that girl again.

And I fear that would kill me.

§

Pulling my hair back into a loose ponytail, I look at my reflection in the mirror and smile for the first time in a long time. I'm happy with what I see. My cheeks don't look hollow, my eyes are bright, and my smile is genuine.

Between work and hanging out with Lindsey, I'm starting to find the girl I had hidden away for years. Garret helps too. I've only seen him a couple times in the last two weeks, but he's been busy working, and well, I'm a coward.

The time I spent with him after he helped me move was terrifying. First I let my guard down enough to actually get into a car with him and not panic over it. Then I agreed to be his friend, and I even accepted his phone number. I haven't used it, but somehow having it makes me feel safer. More comfortable. The one thing I've learned the most about Garret is that I'm safe with him, not just because of his badge but his heart.

Forcing thoughts of Garret from my head, I shut the bathroom light and, after grabbing my purse from my bed, head off for work. I'm tired, the nightmare chasing away sleep for the remainder of the night. I'd made myself a pot of coffee and grabbed the latest Nora Roberts book, letting her latest romantic trysts chase away the memories of Graham.

Shutting myself into my car, I make the short drive to work and turn into the already half full parking lot. It's gonna be a busy night, I can already tell. But busy means it'll keep my mind off everything, and hopefully tonight I'll actually be able to sleep.

§

"Hey, girl, can you grab table three for me?" Caroline gives me a pleading look, arms loaded with plates.

I nod, walking over to the table. An older gentleman with longer, graying hair is sitting alone.

"Hello, I'm Nacole and I'll be taking care of you

tonight. Can I start you with a drink?"

"Yes, ma'am. I'll take a draft, whatever you suggest. My nephew is meeting me here soon, so I'll get an IPA for him as well. Also, could I go ahead and order food now?"

Nodding, I pull out my notepad and fix him with a smile. "Absolutely. What can I put in for you guys?"

Order in hand, I head back to the kitchen, tacking the slip up on the post. Turning around, I go back to the bar to grab his drinks, telling Brody what he asked for. He fills a glass of one of the IPAs and pushes it toward me with a smile.

"No Linds tonight?" I ask.

Brody shakes his head. "Nope. She's at the hospital until eleven, and with an early shift tomorrow, I won't be seeing her until I head home myself."

"Oh, that's too bad." I take the glass from the bar and grab a few napkins, taking everything over to table three and placing it down in front of the customer. He declines when I ask if he needs anything else for the moment, and I head over to another of my tables to check in.

Fifteen minutes later, I hear the bell ding from the kitchen, signaling table three's order is up. Grabbing the two plates with burgers and fries, I'm carrying it to the table just as someone sits across from the older man.

Holy shit.

Even with a Red Sox cap pulled down low on his head, the dark hair peeking out and the tattoos winding around his toned arms tell me I'm looking right at the lead singer of the country band Dark Roads. Chris Hines.

Holy. Shit.

Setting the plates in front of them, I make eye contact with him and my cheeks heat. Tucking a loose strand of hair behind my ear, I turn around and hurry off. Finding Caroline standing out back by the kitchen, I can't help my shriek of excitement.

"You'll never guess who's out there at my table."

"No idea. Who?"

Black hair bobbing around her shoulders, she turns to grab a serving tray, turning back to me with a questioning look.

"Chris Hines!"

"Oh, is he here again?"

"Again? This is a recurring thing?"

Caroline laughs. "Girl, he's friends with Brody. They were all in here last year after a show downtown. He's known Cooper Hall for years."

"Shut up. Holy shit, I just met my first celebrity and I acted like a dunce."

"Please, those guys are far from celebrities. They're the most down-to-earth people you'll ever meet. Seriously."

Grabbing plates, she loads the tray and is gone with a wink, heading out to serve whatever table she's taking care of.

Hearing the front door bell jingle, I head out onto the floor to greet whoever just came in. Garret and Jace stand in front of the door, both dressed in jeans and a T-shirt. My cheeks heat again this time, but not for the same reason as before. I haven't seen Garret since last week, nor have I spoken to him. I think he expected me to call him when he gave me his number, but I didn't.

Garret gives me a giant smile, and when I reach them, he moves to hug me and I brace myself. Instead, he leans down and drops a kiss to my cheek. Jace gives me a smile as well, and I offer them a booth on the side of the bar, close to where my other tables are. Knowing what they both like to drink, I head over to the bar and have Brody pour them.

After I give them their beverages, I sidle back over to where Chris and his uncle are sitting, tension lining their bodies. It looks to be a heated conversation, and I carefully approach the table, not wanting to interrupt.

"Another?" I ask, reaching for the empty glasses.

With a smile, Chris nods at me, and I slide them from the table, heading back to the bar. The door jingles with a new customer, and I look up to see a large man with facial hair and a pissed-off expression step inside.

Yeah, not dealing with him. I don't like angry men.

Looking away from him, I'm reaching out to put the glass on top of the bar when I'm roughly shoved to the side, the glass falling to the floor and shattering into pieces. My knees hit the floor with a painful thud, and I clench my eyes shut.

I'm helpless against the images of Graham roughly playing across my mind. Gulping in a breath, I can't control my breathing.

My eyes open and I turn to see a brawl behind me, the man who pushed me raining punches down on Chris.

Tears sting my eyes, and I watch in horror as Garret and Jace jump into action.

Just as the man cocks his arm back to deliver another blow, Garret grabs his outstretched arm and wrenches it back, the man struggling against him.

"You may want to think twice about that, pal. I'm an off-duty officer." Garret hauls his ass from the bar as the guy continues to spit profanities at him and Chris.

As he pulls the guy to the door, Garret looks to Brody over the bar.

"Can you call the cops, man? Jace drove, and I don't have cuffs on me. That guy's bleeding like a fucker too. He needs to be checked out."

Garret must not notice me, because he doesn't even hesitate before hauling the guy out.

Carefully, I try to get to my feet, but a sharp pain in my hand has me crying out. *Shit.* Looking down, I see a small slice on my palm. A trickle of blood falls down my hand and a tear escapes.

Clenching my eyes shut, I have to count to ten, trying to calm my breathing. When I reach seven, I feel hands come down on my bare arms and I jump, feeling the sting in my palm.

I find myself face-to-face with Brody, his eyebrows knit in concern. Carefully, he helps me stand up and looks at the cut. Grabbing for a towel on the bar, he presses it to my hand.

"You okay?" he asks me softly, but I can't answer. Pulling the towel back, he examines my hand, then looks up at me with a smile. "You're lucky. This shouldn't need stitches. It doesn't look too deep."

As I stare at my feet, he tends to my hand, and in minutes I hear sirens wailing outside. Through the large window, I watch Garret forcing the guy over to a patrol car, the guy struggling the entire time. Noise around me is fading and I close my eyes, fighting off the looming panic attack.

"Nacole!" Brody's voice booms and I jump, startled by the harshness of his voice.

"I'm sorry," he says, wrapping an arm around my shoulders, trying to keep me steady. "I asked you three times if you were hurt anywhere else, and you're starting to freak me out."

"I'm fine," I whisper as EMTs come into the bar. One heads straight for Chris, and the other comes over to us.

"You okay, ma'am?"

Brody pulls the towel off my hand and the guy goes about looking at the wound. I just want to leave. I need the safety of my home.

Reaching into his bag, the man bandages my hand up and then heads over to where Chris and the other EMT are. Jace is still over there, and when I dare to turn my head, I'm horrified to see how badly Chris is hurt.

Placing a towel to his forehead, they help him out of the bar, my eyes wide in fright. Brody never leaves my side, and after they have Chris loaded up, he walks me out back to his office, helping me sit down.

"Nacole, you're really spooking me here. Are you

okay?"

Shaking my head, I fold over in the chair and start to bawl, both from the fear I felt earlier and the embarrassment of my behavior. I'm a total wack job, and now everyone knows it.

Brody excuses himself for a second, and I try like hell to get it together. But I lose the battle when I look up through my tears to find Garret standing there, a sad smile on his face.

"Hey, you," he says, and in seconds I'm off the chair and burying my face in his neck, his strong arms coming around me in comfort. "Shh, it's okay. Are you all right?"

Shaking my head, I cling to him as he moves us farther into the room so he can shut the door behind us.

Pulling away, he carefully wipes my tears with the back of his hand.

"You know, darlin', we really need to stop meeting like this," he jokes, and I can't help it. Somehow it breaks the cloud I've been in and I start laughing, his own husky chuckle in my ear.

"I'm so sorry," I tell him, sitting down in the chair again.

Kneeling in front of me, he takes my injured hand and presses a soft kiss to the bandage.

"That's better. I prefer your laugh to your tears," he says.

"You and me both," I groan.

In moments, Garret Walker has cast aside the shadows of my past.

And he doesn't even know it.

CHAPTER SIX

GARRET

Well that sure as hell wasn't how my night off was supposed to go.

When Jace and I decided to go to Walker's, I honestly just wanted a beer and something greasy to eat. We had a long shift, filled with one stupid asshole after another, and I couldn't hide my excitement when Nacole came walking over to us. I wasn't sure if she was working, but I was awfully happy to see she was.

After giving us our beers, she walked away, and my eyes stayed trained on that ass. I swear it would fill my hands perfectly. Jace gave me shit and I stopped staring at her, at least to stop having to listen to him.

But then the night went to shit when that asshole decided to attack a music superstar. From what I understand, Chris isn't pressing charges, so he'll probably be let off with some bullshit misdemeanor charge.

Once I finished explaining the situation to another officer, I was heading back inside when Brody came walking out from his office, an unreadable expression on his face. After he told me that Nacole had completely fallen apart in there, I pushed past him and went straight for her.

She went home early, not long after I finished seeing to her. Brody told her not to worry about it and he'd see her the next day. I watched her leave before heading back to my evening with Jace, though I haven't been able to stop thinking about her.

I'm pulled from my thoughts when Caroline walks over to the table.

"You guys want another round?" she asks, and we both shake our heads. Two is Jace's limit when he's driving, and I'm not in the mood anymore.

Nodding, she clears away the empty glasses and plates, coming back a few minutes later with the check. I tell Jace I got it tonight and hand her my debit card.

While we're waiting, Jace leans forward and folds his arms together on the table.

"What?" I ask.

"So, you and this Nacole chick, huh?"

I laugh. "'Nacole chick'? It's just Nacole, man. And we aren't anything. We're just friends."

"That's what they all say, buddy."

"Yeah, the only difference is I'm dead serious. We're friends. Drop it, Miller."

Jace shakes his head at me as Caroline comes back over with the receipt and my card. I scribble my name and a tip and hand the slip back with a smile.

Waving to my brother as we're walking out, we head to Jace's truck and climb in.

He turns to me, his face serious. "I'm just saying, Garret. She seems to have no interest in anybody or anything, but she's different with you. And you're different with her."

"I am?" I put my seat belt on and he starts the truck, driving to my house.

"Yeah, man. I can't put my finger on it, but you are. I've known you for how long? Ridden besides you for a decade, longer even. I'm just waiting to see how long it takes before you both realize it and pull your heads from your asses."

The rest of the drive is silent, and when we pull into my driveway, I bump his fist and climb out, heading straight inside. Locking the front door behind me, I drop my wallet and keys on the entry table and go to my bedroom. Plugging my cell in, I'm unbuttoning my jeans when my phone beeps with a text.

Unknown: Thank you for tonight, Garret.

Garret: Nacole?

Unknown: Yeah.

I quickly save her number into my phone before replying.

Garret: You feeling better?

Nacole: Yeah, I am. I appreciate you being so kind.

Garret: That's just the kinda man I am.

Nacole: I think I've figured that out.

Smirking, I kick my pants off before climbing into my bed. Reaching for the remote on my end table, I switch on the end of the Braves game and settle back. Only a few minutes have passed when my phone chimes again.

Nacole: Do you think I could call you?

Garret: Now? Yeah, sure.

Waiting for my phone to light up with a call, I lower the volume on my TV. I'm shocked when a second later I receive an incoming FaceTime alert. Holding it up in front of my face, I hit Accept, and then I'm staring into those beautiful brown eyes.

"Hey," I greet, giving her a large smile. I can't handle how adorable she is when she waves at me, a tiny smile pulling at the corners of her mouth.

"Hi. Sorry if this is bad timing. I didn't even think to ask if you were still out."

"Nah, you're fine. Got home a few minutes ago."

Nodding, she tucks her hair behind her ear and chews on a fingernail. "I just got a new phone this morning, and I wanted to try out this app."

"Ah, well feel free to video-call me all you want. I'm completely down with being your guinea pig," I joke. Sitting up straighter, I tuck my arm behind my head and get comfortable.

"Plus, I mean, you are quite handsome. I was okay

with getting to see you again."

Well damn. Someone's starting to get comfortable with me.

"Oh really?" I quip, raising an eyebrow.

She lets out a little giggle and I laugh with her, glad she's finally starting to let those walls down.

"Oh gosh, I can't believe I actually said that. I'm sorry." Her cheeks darken and I smile.

"Don't be. I like sassy Nacole. She's pretty cute."

Nacole blushes even harder and I love it. I'm trying to wrap my head around the fact that this is the same girl from earlier. So confident, so relaxed, so fucking beautiful. She has on absolutely no makeup, her hair down around her shoulders. I can't help wondering if it's as soft as it looks.

"You're not so bad yourself."

"Thank you. So, you doing okay? You really had Brody and me worried earlier."

"Yeah, that's actually the reason I called you, Garret." Her face takes on a serious look and she sighs, brushing her hair off her shoulders. "I know it's so silly, but that guy freaked me out. I don't know, it was like I was locked in this bubble, and my brain couldn't push past the fear I felt when he shoved me over."

"Seriously, you don't need to apologize, I get it. I see so much shit every time I'm on the clock that nothing fazes me anymore. But I understand where you're coming from. That guy was huge and strong, and he really did a number on Hines. Would've freaked anyone out."

"I appreciate you saying that. Really."

"Of course."

An awkward silence hits, and I just sit there staring at her.

What the hell is it about this girl? Shit, is Jace right? Do I like her? No, I don't. Hell, I don't even know anything about her beyond her name and job, and where she lives. That's all.

"So, tell me all about Nacole Ward."

"Nothing really to tell. I'm a waitress."

"Bullshit. There has to be something you want to share with me."

Nacole bites down on her bottom lip in thought, and then a huge smile a mile wide spreads across her face. "I can make deep-fried Oreos, I know how to crochet, I can—"

I hold a hand up. "Stop. Repeat what you just said."

"I can crochet."

"No, before that."

She raises an eyebrow. "I can make deep-fried Oreos?"

"Yeah, that. Tell me more about that."

"Uh, they're chocolate sandwich cookies—"

"No, I mean tell me when you can make them and I'm there. Literally."

Throwing her head back, she laughs loudly, and I love every second of it. "God, what are you, five? They're not *that* special."

"I'm gonna pretend you didn't just say that."

Laughing harder, she wipes a tear from her face and

shakes her head at me. "Garret Walker, what am I going to do with you?"

"Take me on a date?" I say, surprising even myself.

Her eyes almost pop out of her head, but I see a trace of a smile.

"No, thank you. But nice try."

Both laughing, we talk for a little while longer before ending the call to go to bed. Long after we say good night, I'm left reeling over her.

Yeah, friends, my ass. I like her, and I'll be damned if I don't at least try to get her. No matter how long it takes.

§

"Walker, you got a second?" Looking up from my desk, Jonah Clarke, the station's sergeant, is in front of me, smile on his face.

"Sure, what's up, Sarge?"

"So, a little birdie told me you're taking the detective's exam this fall?"

"Shit." Standing from my desk, I move around it so I'm in front of him. "I've been meaning to tell you. I just didn't want to make a big thing of it."

He holds a hand up, stopping me from continuing, then extends it to me. I shake it and he smiles at me again.

"It's about damn time, Walker." My eyebrows shoot up in shock, and he chuckles. "Garret, you're a damn fine cop. One of the best we have in this district, and I'm glad to see you using that talent towards furthering your career. Best of luck, son."

He strolls away, leaving me with my jaw hanging open. Somehow I force myself to get rid of the shit-eating grin on my face. Sergeant Clarke doesn't dish out compliments to just anyone. He's a good guy, but he's also a hard-ass on everyone in the department.

Broken from my thoughts by my ringing phone, I glance down at the screen and see it's Brody. Answering, I sit back down, getting comfortable. "Hey, bro."

"Garret, glad I caught you. Listen, are you busy tonight?"

"No, I'm off work in just a couple hours. Why, what's up?"

"Linds wanted to throw a get-together, and like my lovely wife always does, it's last fucking minute."

Laughing, I nod in understanding. "Yeah, that does sound like her. What time? I'll be there."

"Five? I'm inviting Hunter and Grayson too. Noah and Chase have some family dinner tonight."

"Sounds good, man. I'll see you then."

"Oh, one other thing." There's a hint of laughter in Brody's voice, and I brace myself for whatever stupidity he has up his sleeve.

"What?"

"Lindsey wants Nacole there. Invite her? Thanks, see you tonight." Brody ends the call and I'm left cursing him out.

Fucker knows exactly what he's doing.

It takes all of five minutes to follow through with what

he asked. Clearly he and my sister-in-law are playing matchmaker, but they don't seem to realize that this isn't exactly a chore for me. I'd love nothing more than to see her tonight.

Pulling up her number, I hit Call and hold my breath, waiting for her to answer.

CHAPTER SEVEN

NACOLE

I pace my small living room, wringing my hands together. *This was a bad idea. I shouldn't have agreed to this.* Garret called me a couple of hours ago, asking if I would go with him to a party at Brody's. Said it wasn't him asking me out, that it was as friends, and they all wanted me there. I agreed, and I've spent the last two hours questioning that decision.

Dressed in a navy cotton dress and a pair of flats, I left my hair down, no makeup on. Not that I'd brought any with me, even if I wanted to wear it. Graham always insisted I was done up to the nines everywhere we went, saying I looked better that way. Now I hate makeup and relish the fact that I never have to wear it if I don't want to.

Heading back into my kitchen, I grab a bottle of water and down half of it in a few gulps, hands shaking. I shouldn't be nervous, but I am.

Sitting down at the tiny table I bought earlier this week, I take a few deeps breaths, trying to reassure myself.

You know Garret.

He's a good guy.

You're safe with him.

Brody is your boss.

You're safe.

When there's a knock at my front door, I look out the peephole to see Garret standing there, hands in his front pockets. Letting out a sigh of relief, I unlock the several locks and pull the door open. Dressed in a pair of tight jeans, boots, and a gray shirt, he's out-of-this-world gorgeous.

His curly hair has been cut recently, brushed back and off his face. His blue eyes bore into mine, lips turned up in a smile as he takes me in.

"What?" I ask, brushing my hair off my shoulders.

"You look beautiful," he states, and my cheeks heat at the compliment.

Reaching over to the couch for my purse, I step outside and close the door behind me, locking it tight.

"Let's roll, darlin'."

Walking me over to the passenger side of his Jeep, he opens the door for me and I hop inside, pulling the seat belt over me. Garret climbs in and does his own buckle, turning to me with a smile.

"What?" I ask again, raising an eyebrow at him.

"Nothing. I'm just really glad you're coming tonight is all."

"Me too," I tell him honestly.

Starting the engine, he backs out of my driveway and we're on our way. The drive is short, country music playing quietly in the background. He tells me we're almost there, and I lean forward to turn up the music. Blake Shelton has always been one of my favorites, and this song is one of my most adored songs. Singing along quietly, I almost miss Garret staring over at me while we wait for the stoplight. When we pull into Brody's driveway a few minutes later, he parks and turns to me.

"So, remember how I said you needed to see a concert?"

"Yeah, I do. Why?"

"Well, I got us tickets to that festival I was talking about. It's next Thursday."

"Okay?"

Garret shakes his head at me, chuckling. "I'm taking you, okay?"

"We'll see, buddy."

Climbing down, I shut the door behind me and come around the hood, Garret meeting me halfway. He offers me his arm and I laugh, linking mine through his. His warm skin against mine has butterflies dancing in my stomach, and my skin prickles. His left hand comes down to cover mine and we walk inside.

"Hey, fucker, we're here!" he shouts, and I look at him in surprise.

"Garret, that's not exactly the kindest way to introduce us," I gasp.

He laughs loudly. "Just you wait."

Brody strolls in a second later, beer bottle in hand. "Hey, twatsicle. Glad you could grace us with your not-so-lovely presence."

Garret lets go of my arm and steps toward Brody, grabbing him into a headlock. They horse around for just a moment, and then Garret drapes his arm around his brother's shoulders, looking at me with a grin.

"Nacole, glad you came," Brody says. I thank him as Garret reaches out for me.

Excusing us, I follow him out back to the kitchen, where a large porch is attached. We step outside to the deck and find everyone waiting on us. Music is playing from a set of speakers, and I see Lindsey down on the grass, talking to another set of couples.

Garret offers me a beer and I shake my head. I haven't touched alcohol in years, and I don't plan to. Alcohol makes people angry, and anger leads to hurt. I don't ever want to turn into somebody I'm not—I already have a hard enough time just being me. He offers me a soda from the cooler and I take it with a smile, following him down to where everyone is.

"Nacole!" Lindsey shrieks, and I laugh when she bolts over to me, giving me a hard hug. Leaving her arm around my shoulders, she walks me over to everyone. "Girl, this is Hunter Daniels and his wife, Carmen. And that's Grayson Michaels and his wife, Kennedy."

They all wave and say hello, and I do the same, slightly intimidated. Their wives are drop-dead gorgeous, and

Grayson is huge, at least six-four. No part of me fits in here, but they all seem nice and I tell myself to relax. This could be a lot of fun if I could just calm down and stop overthinking things.

Taking a sip of my drink, I follow Lindsey and the other girls to a table they have set up. Settling into a chair, I look over my shoulder, finding Garret watching me with a smile. He winks and I flush before turning to face the girls.

"Oh, girl. That guy is just smitten with you," Lindsey giggles, and I shake my head.

"We're just friends," I concede, running my finger around the top of the can.

"For now," Kennedy jokes.

I smile, but in my head I disagree.

Just friends. That's all we'll ever be.

§

I'm so glad I stepped out of my comfort zone and came tonight. I've been having the most amazing time, and everyone here is awesome. I really jive well with the girls, and they've kept me plenty entertained telling me stories about their husbands. We've eaten dinner, and now the guys are down in the backyard playing cornhole while us girls lounge by the table, watching them and chatting up a storm.

Carmen is next to me, and she and I get along best. I really like her, and I'm drawn to her. I haven't the faintest clue why, but she reminds me so much of myself. Plus, we're about the same age.

"So, how did you all meet?" I ask, folding my legs under me.

"Well," Kennedy starts, "I met Gray when our best friends started dating. That would be Noah and Aubrey. Noah is Carmen's older brother, and they're all firefighters a couple towns over."

"I met Hunter a few months after I moved home from college. I was working in a bakery a couple streets over from the firehouse when he came in to get breakfast for the guys." Carmen reaches for the bottle of wine on the table and pours herself a glass.

"They met Brody when they started frequenting Walker's," Lindsey says.

"They seem great," I tell them, and their eyes light up when they look over at the guys.

Garret has kept his distance from me since we got here, respecting my space, and I can't help feel a twinge of jealousy at these women. Not only are they all smart and beautiful, but they have incredible men, and happy lives. It wasn't something I ever thought I would want again, but sitting here now, I realize I do. And I think I want that with Garret. But that's too big a risk for me. What if we get close and he changes? What if he hurts me?

I can't bear that again.

Years with Graham led to my lack of self-esteem, and while I know deep down that I'm not a horrible choice, I feel like Garret deserves better than me. Someone who can be honest with him, not hold him back from a full life.

Kennedy and Lindsey excuse themselves, running down to join the guys. Watching Grayson sweep Kennedy into his arms, grabbing her ass, a mist fills my eyes. My brain can't figure out why my heart is sad, so I turn away, finding Carmen looking at me.

"You okay?" she asks, and I nod with a smile, forcing the tears away.

"Yeah. I'm having a lot of fun with you guys."

"I'm glad. We're a crazy bunch, but you won't find anyone who will love you more."

"I see that." As I reach for my water, a hand comes down on my shoulder and I jump, throwing the water away from me.

"Shit." Garret kneels next to me, eyes filled with concern.

"Jesus, Garret," I groan, hand over my pounding heart.

"I'm sorry," he says, giving me an apologetic smile.

"You scared the hell out of me," I tell him, reaching over to slap his shoulder.

Laughing, he jumps up and retrieves my water, handing it to me. I'm tempted to pour it over his head, but he jogs over to the cooler to get more beers, taking them down to the others.

Shaking my head and all thoughts of terror away, I turn to Carmen to find her looking at me, her eyes sad and wide.

"What?" I ask.

"How long?" She moves her chair closer to mine.

"How long what?"

"How long did he hurt you?"

I'm completely taken aback, mouth dropping open and eyes welling with tears.

"I don't know what you're—"

"Nacole, it's okay. I know. I've been there."

Well I didn't expect that.

"Seven years," I whisper, and her eyes widen in shock before she leans forward to give me a hug. When she pulls away, I see tears sparkling in her eyes.

"When did you leave?"

"Four months ago. Moved down here and was living in this run-down apartment. Spent the first few months crying and sleeping. I lost my mom back in January, and I never got a chance…"

It all comes out like word vomit, and I watch Carmen's expression switch from shock to sadness, to anger and then back to sadness.

She reaches out for my hand and gives it a squeeze. "I'm so sorry, girl. How are you doing now?"

"Honestly? Better than I have in a long time. Losing Mom was my breaking point with Graham, and every day, I feel better. I feel like myself."

"Good."

"Can I ask you something, Carmen?"

"Of course."

"What gave it away?"

She sighs. "I saw the flash of fear in your eyes when Garret scared you. It's only noticeable to the group of us who have been through it. The six months that Craig hurt me were the hardest and most painful months of my life, and I don't mean just physically but emotionally. He tried to kill me in the end, and every day, when I see Hunter, or I wake up and get annoyed because I didn't get enough sleep, I remember. I remember having final thoughts. I was only twenty-two years old, but I knew my life hadn't been enough for me. I wanted more out of it."

I nod, knowing exactly what she means. "Graham wasn't always physical. I mean, here and there over the first couple years, but it was his words that hurt the most. I was worthless. Why did he bother marrying me? I was a waste of his time. Holding him back." Shaking off the nightmares, I forge ahead. "He became more physical with me the last couple years. That's around the time he started sleeping with his assistants, and anyone else he could get his hands on."

"Asshole," Carmen grumbles, smiling when I laugh at her.

"I don't know why, but after Mom died, it became so much worse. She was all I had, and it was like he knew he didn't have to hold back anymore, that he could do whatever he wanted. It was like he didn't care if anyone could see the bruises anymore."

"Nacole..."

"I left him, and every single day I've spent in Tennessee has been lighter and happier than I've been in a long time. While I never expected being almost thirty with a bachelor's degree yet working in a sports bar to be fulfilling, it is. I enjoy working at the bar. I'm trying to make friends and carve out a life here. Garret has just been the wrench that I can't decide what to do with."

"You like him." It's not a question, and I smile at Carmen.

"Yeah, I do. But I don't want to date him, because that leads to a relationship and that could wind up being my downfall."

"Or it could be the best thing to happen to you." Carmen moves her chair so she's in front of me, taking both of my hands in hers.

"Can I tell you something?"

"Of course."

Biting her lower lip, she looks past me to Hunter, and I see her eyes light up, the happiness and love behind them. "I met Hunter when I was at my lowest point. Nightmares on an almost nightly basis. I lost someone I cared about, and he was there for me. No questions asked, no expectations. But it was my fear that drove us apart. And while temporary, it was enough."

"I'm sorry." I feel a tear escape down my cheek and I swipe it away.

"I'm not saying you and Garret are meant to drive off into the sunset together, but you like him, and I think he likes you too. Don't let a monster like Graham determine the rest of your life. Don't let him take any more happiness away from you. You deserve more than that."

Her words strike a chord with me and I look over my shoulder to where Garret is. He's unaware of my gaze, and I watch as he laughs over something Brody says to him, head thrown back and mouth open wide. A smile creeps across my face and I look back to Carmen.

"Thank you," I tell her sincerely.

"Hey, what are friends for?" With a short squeeze, she brushes past me to go down to Hunter, who instantly grabs her for a kiss.

Decision made, I stand up and brush off my dress. Squaring my shoulders, I walk down to join everyone.

Carmen is right. Graham is my past. I have no idea if Garret is my future, but I'll be damned if I spend another second living in the past.

It's time to start living for today.

CHAPTER EIGHT

GARRET

"So, when are you and Jace gonna fess up to being 'partner' partners?" Hunter jokes, tossing the beanbag to me, my turn up next.

"Dude, shut up," I groan, hefting the beanbag at Hunter's head. Laughing, he takes a swig of his beer and picks the beanbag up, throwing it back at me.

"What? It was an innocent question."

"Yeah, but it came out of *your* stupid-ass mouth, so it wasn't innocent."

"I'll take that as a yes, then," he laughs, and this time I get him in the stomach with the beanbag. With an "oof," he falls to the ground. "Hey, take it easy. You bruised my eight-pack, man!"

"What fucking eight-pack?" Grayson taunts and Hunter jumps up.

"Wanna see?"

"Hunter, put your shirt down," Carmen exclaims, rushing over to join us.

"Busted!" I shout, laughing loudly.

Hunter grabs Carmen for a kiss and I turn to find Nacole walking toward us, a smile on her face. Every time I see it, I swear it takes my breath away. She is so goddamn beautiful, and she really has no idea.

"Hey, you," I greet, thrown for a loop when she walks into my arms, giving me a tight hug. I pull her to me and she tucks her face into my neck.

"Thank you," she whispers.

"For what?"

Nacole lifts her head and has an even bigger smile on her face, her eyes sparkling. "For bringing me tonight. I really needed this."

"I'm real glad to hear it."

She moves so she's next to me and I sling my arm around her, pulling her close to me. I don't miss the way her arm curls around my waist, or how she rests her head on my shoulder.

And I definitely don't miss how fucking perfect she fits with me.

§

"Thank you, guys, for coming. It was so much fun." Lindsey hugs me tight and I hold her to me before pulling back. Then she and Nacole hug and she whispers something in Nacole's ear, who starts giggling at her.

I clap Brody on the back, and then we head around the house to my Jeep, the sun having set long ago.

Helping her in, I shut the door behind her and go around the hood, climbing into my side. Turning the key, I back out of my brother's driveway and take off. The windows are down and the radio is cranked, Brett Eldridge singing something about being drunk and in love. The wind is blowing Nacole's long hair all over the place, and she's singing off-key at the top of her lungs, a huge smile on her face. The glow from the dashboard lights up her face and I smile, wishing I could record the moment.

When I pull into her driveway ten minutes later, I kill the engine and turn to her. "Thank you for coming tonight."

"Thank you for asking. Seriously, Garret, that was the best night I've had in a long time. I really like your friends."

"Well they're your friends now too."

"I know."

With a laugh, she climbs out of my Jeep and I follow her, walking her to the front door. I step onto the small porch behind her, watching her fumble with her keys beneath the outdoor light. Finding the right one, she unlocks the door and tosses the keys in her purse.

"Well, thank you again."

"You're welcome."

With my hands in my pockets, I look down at her in the dim light as she chews her lower lip. Before I get a chance to ask what's on her mind, she stands on tiptoes and gently presses her lips to mine. I don't get a chance to kiss her back before she pulls away, eyes wide at her forwardness.

Now it's my turn.

Cradling her face, I kiss her again, holding her body to mine. Her small hands grip my biceps, her soft lips warm against mine. Groaning, I deepen the kiss and gently demand access with my tongue. The second she accepts, I tangle mine with hers, capturing her quiet moans with my mouth.

The kiss becomes heated, and I carefully back her up against her house, my cock completely at attention and ready to go. Nacole runs her hands down my arms until they're wrapped around my waist. My heart is pounding, and my skin feels like it's been touched with a live wire.

I fucking want her more than I've ever wanted anyone.

But I force myself to calm down, and with a final brush of my tongue against hers, I place one last kiss to her swollen mouth and pull back. Her eyes are heavy lidded with desire, her mouth turned up into a small smile.

"Why'd you stop?" she whispers, she's looking up at me.

"Because I'll be damned if the first time I get to kiss you, it ends with me taking you against the side of your house."

"Oh."

"Look at me, sweetheart." Tipping her face up to mine, I drop a kiss to her forehead. "I like you, Nacole, but I refuse to rush anything with you. I can tell you're still scared, and I'll wait for as long as you need, because I don't want to scare you or force you into something you aren't ready for."

With a smile, she leans up and kisses my scruffy cheek. "Good night, Garret."

"I'll call you."

Without another word, I stroll to my Jeep, willing my stupid fucking dick to calm down. When it doesn't, I groan, starting the vehicle.

"Better get used to being blue, fucker."

§

Stepping from the shower, I quickly dry off and wrap a towel around my waist, then go over to the mirror, wiping the steam from it. Grabbing my electric razor, I quickly clean up my scruff before brushing my teeth. I glance into my bedroom at the clock on the wall, seeing I need to leave in twenty minutes.

It's been a week since the party my brother threw, and I haven't seen Nacole since. We've talked every day though, and I'm happy that today is the country festival, if for no other reason than I get to spend the entire day with her. She still has no idea who we're seeing, and I can't wait to see her face.

Briskly towel-drying my hair, I toss the bath sheets in the basket and head into my room to get dressed. Throwing on my favorite jeans and a T-shirt, I look around my room, finally finding my worn Braves cap. Jamming it on my head, I grab a pair of socks and sneakers, heading for my living room. The smell of coffee fills the area, and after tying my laces, I make my way to the kitchen, filling a travel mug with coffee, black. Shoving the tickets in my wallet, I head out for my Jeep, coffee in hand. It's only ten thirty, and the concert isn't set to start until seven, but I made sure to make plans to fill our day.

As I make the drive to Nacole's, I drink my coffee, glad I took the top off my Jeep. It's an absolutely gorgeous day out, and I know it's going to be an amazing day for her.

Pulling into her driveway, I finish my coffee and stick it in the cupholder. She's sitting on her front steps, reading some paperback. She looks up and smiles, waving at me.

Today just got a whole lot more gorgeous.

§

Hand in hand, we're walking through downtown Nashville, Nacole's eyes huge as she takes in all the sights. Dressed in jean shorts and a white shirt, I haven't been able to take my eyes off her. She's every bit the little country fan at the moment, and I love it. Unable to resist, I pull my cell from my back pocket and hold it up, telling her to smile. She does at the same time a breeze blows, her hair in her face and smile bright.

It's time for us to head to the concert, so I take her hand once more and walk us back to my Jeep. I can't help leaning down to kiss her, heart soaring when she laughs against my mouth.

"Just tell me who it is," she pouts.

I chuckle, holding the door open for her. "No chance, babe."

I pull out into traffic, and she leans over and turns the radio on. I can't help the smirk when she turns up the latest Blake Shelton single, but my excitement dies a second later when the song ends and the radio host starts talking.

"And that was the latest single from Blake Shelton, who'll be live in Nashville tonight—"

I reach over to change stations, but I'm not fast enough. Nacole is looking at me with her mouth open wide, her eyes bright and excited.

"Garret?"

I let out a deep sigh. "Yes, we're seeing Blake Shelton."

With a loud whoop, she surprises me when she leans across the seat and kisses me on the cheek before pulling away with a fist pump.

"Well, now that the surprise is ruined," I groan.

"No it's not. I am so excited."

"I couldn't tell," I joke. My surprise may be shot, but it's nothing compared to the happiness on her face. And I'm the one who did that.

Tonight is gonna fucking rock.

§

Halfway through the concert, this is easily a night for

the books. I got us pit tickets, so we're standing in a crowd of people, Nacole in front of me. We've been dancing and singing all night, and now Blake is currently crooning out the ballad "God Gave Me You."

As much as I would like to pull her into my arms and hold her close, I'm not sure she wants that. She's kept a distance between us since the show started, so I settle for placing my hands on her shoulders. Halfway through the song, she leans back against me, not stopping me when my hands drift down to her waist. The sweet scent of her shampoo fills the air between us and together we dance the night away, not a care in the world.

§

"Call me tomorrow, okay?"

"You know I will." Giving her a kiss on the cheek, I force myself to turn around and walk away, hearing her front door close behind her. Climbing into the Jeep, I turn the headlights on and crank the engine, heading back to my house. It's well after midnight and I'm ready to crash. The rest of the concert was amazing and we lingered on the way home, grabbing an ice cream cone to share. I felt like a teenager all night, and I've never seen her so happy and relaxed.

It was the best night ever. Her words, not mine, but I have to agree.

Pulling into my driveway a few minutes later, I don't bother putting the cover back on the Jeep before I head inside. Five minutes later, I'm stripping down and climbing into bed. Reaching over, I plug my cell phone in and notice a text waiting for me.

Nacole: Tonight was magical. Thank you.

Garret: You're welcome. We'll have to go to another sometime.

Nacole: Definitely. But this time I'll plan the surprise.

Garret: You're on.

Locking my phone screen, I set it on my nightstand and lie down, getting comfortable. Sleep doesn't elude me for long, and when I do, I dream about a long-haired brunette, dancing her way into my heart.

CHAPTER NINE

NACOLE

Nightmares plagued my sleep last night. I have one normal day, one day where I can be myself and start to feel like maybe this could be my life, and then Graham is right there, making sure I don't get it. That my happiness stays far away.

Pouring myself another cup of coffee, my phone beeps, alerting me to another text message. I've avoided Garret long enough, so I reach across my counter and hold it up.

Garret: Are you working tonight?

Nacole: Yeah, at 6.

Garret: I'm pulling a double. Someone called in sick.

Nacole: Oh no. That stinks.

Garret: Jace is driving me nuts.

Nacole: Sorry :(

Garret: So, I was thinking. Dinner this weekend?

Nacole: I'll let you know.

Moving my phone to the side, I drink my coffee in silence, trying to decide what to do. Last night was amazing. Not only was getting to see my favorite musician in concert incredible, but the company was just as great. Garret was a perfect gentleman all night, holding my hand and keeping me away from drunk concert-goers. I kept telling myself it's just because he's a cop, that he's used to these types of situations, but deep down, the reason had nothing to do with his job.

Garret likes me—it's obvious in the way he looks at me, the way he treats me. But it's hard for me to believe he's as amazing as he seems. Graham was kind and loving to me in the beginning too. I trusted him, and he shattered that trust during our marriage. Now I'm stuck, my brain and my heart wanting two different things. I want to move on, to be happy, but I can't risk my heart. I can't risk my whole self.

If Garret hurt me, it would completely destroy everything I'm working so hard to get back.

And I'm not sure it's a risk I want to take.

§

"Hey, girl, come in."

Almost a week later, I'm standing on Carmen's front

step, smiling as she ushers me inside. I didn't take Garret up on his offer of dinner last week, and while he didn't ask why, he seemed disappointed.

I got a call from Mitchell Hale yesterday, and we had a really long talk. I'm finally ready to take the necessary steps to end the chapter I left behind all those months ago.

I know Carmen was never married to her ex, but I need some advice before I file for divorce. Mitchell thinks we can present all the evidence and that will be enough, that I won't have to go home and face him, but I'm scared. And I can't let myself be with Garret until this is all behind me. It's not fair to him.

I follow Carmen into her living room, where it's cozy and warm. A bottle of wine and a couple glasses are on the coffee table, and Hunter pokes his head into the room as we're sitting on the couch.

"Babe, I'm heading out. You ladies have fun tonight, okay?"

"Say hi to your mom for me?" Carmen stands from the couch to give her husband a hug, and I don't miss the look on his face when he pulls her into his arms, the love that surrounds the two of them.

"I love you," he says, and with a wave to me, he's gone, leaving us alone.

Coming back over to the couch, Carmen plops down next to me and pats my knee. "So, now that we finally get to hang out, tell me. How was the concert?"

"It was really good." I start gushing about the show,

laughing when Carmen rolls her eyes at me.

"Well yeah, it was Blake Shelton. There is no such thing as a bad show if he's performing. And you know that is *not* what I was asking."

She pours us both a glass of wine but I shake my head, refusing the drink. With a shrug, she places the extra back down and turns to me.

"I know," I joke, sitting back and tucking my legs under me. "It was a lot of fun, actually. We danced and ate really bad fair food, and he was the perfect date for my very first country show."

"I'm glad, though I sense a 'but' coming."

"But… I've flaked on him this last week. Something felt like it shifted that night and he was ready to ask me out. Well, I guess he technically already asked me out. But you know what I mean."

"He wants you."

"Yeah."

Carmen trains her eyes on me, the faintest smile on her face. "And this is bad how?"

Sighing loudly, I lean back against the couch, resting a foot on the coffee table.

"I've only known him a month and a half, for starters. I'm not even legally divorced yet, and it certainly hasn't been long enough to even entertain dating."

"Says who?"

"Says…." She caught me. I can't help laughing.

"See? There's absolutely no time limit, no law that says you can't move on, find happiness in another person, a new life for yourself."

"I know."

"Nacole..."

"I'm scared, Carmen. And I think I need help."

She leans forward to place her wineglass on the coffee table. "Help?"

"My lawyer wants me to see someone. And he also wants me to report the abuse so the divorce will go through no matter what Graham contests."

"I think that sounds like a great idea. If you'd like, I can give you the name of the woman I went to see after Craig was arrested for attacking me. She was incredibly helpful, and while I only saw her for a couple months, she really helped me."

I smile and nod, eyes misty. Carmen leans over to squeeze my hand, then picks up her glass of wine. "Now, give me all the dirty details about our resident Walker brother."

Laughing, I settle in for a night filled with laughs and memories, ones I never thought I would get again. And surprisingly, I don't feel any heaviness on my chest. Instead, I relish the moment, grateful I found her and finally have someone to confide in.

§

"Graham, you promised," I argue, tossing the dishcloth on the counter.

My husband's green eyes glare at me over the kitchen

island, his body tight and rigid with anger.

"I did not, Sadie. Do not put fucking words in my mouth."

Shaking my head in frustration, I turn away from him. He's hell-bent on ruining tonight for us, and I refuse to let him spoil my mood. We've been married just over a month, and something's wrong. Every night he comes home angry with me for something I didn't do, and every night I go to bed wondering what's changed. What happened to my kind and caring partner?

"I just wanted tonight to be special, Graham. You've been working so hard, and I just wanted to take you somewhere nice."

"Well, unlike you, I work my ass to the bone every single day. Did you ever think that maybe, just maybe, the last thing I want to do when I come home is take your lazy ass out to dinner? Did you ever think that maybe I wanted my wife to get off her ass and have dinner waiting for me? Huh, Sadie?"

His voice grows louder with each word, and I turn around to find him strolling toward me, his face red with anger and the muscles in his neck cording.

"I'm sorry, Graham, I just—"

"Exactly. You just. I didn't marry you to fucking think, I married you because it was easy. Cancel the reservation and make dinner yourself, I have work to do tonight."

Tears spill down my cheeks, and I lift a trembling hand to wipe them away. Graham has never spoken to me like this, and I absolutely refuse to let it happen. Squaring my *shoulders, I walk up to him, hands on my hips.*

"Screw you, Graham. I have no idea what kind of bug is up your ass tonight, but—"

I barely have time to react when he spins around and backhands me right across the face, the harsh sting making me cry out, my hand shooting up to cover the reddening skin he just hit.

"You do not get to talk to me like that. Do I make myself clear?" He spits out the words, and I can do little more than nod, tears falling down my cheeks, each one a small representation of the pain in my heart. Graham stalks away, his office door slamming shut a moment later.

Wiping my tears away, I bustle around the kitchen, doing exactly as he said. In my mind, I plan to pack my suitcase when he leaves in the morning, disgusted with him. How dare he? Not once in the years we've been together has he ever hit me. But he never will again.

I wipe my eyes with a tissue and look up at Dr. Klein, the psychiatrist Carmen told me about. Her warm brown eyes are sad as I recount the first time Graham ever hit me. When I first came in about an hour ago, I couldn't stop twisting my hands together with nerves, but I found myself incredibly comfortable with her. I haven't confided in her about my current situation as much as I would like, but she asked me what I came to talk about and I answered with Graham, so there we have it.

"So, up until then, your husband had never put his hands on you?"

"No."

"Did he ever raise his voice during arguments like that?"

Shrugging, I blow my nose and crumple the tissue in my hand. "I mean, yeah we got into arguments. What couple doesn't? But he'd never treated me that way, and he most certainly never hurt me."

"I'm very sorry you went through that, Nacole."

"Sadie," I tell her, my voice quiet yet steady. She gives me a questioning glare. "My full name is Sadie Nacole Ward. I've been going by my middle name since I moved here."

Dr. Klein nods at me. "As a way of starting over, but not forgetting." It's a statement, not a question, and she couldn't be more correct.

"Nacole was my mom's name. I'm an only child, raised by a single mom. She was my best friend, my entire world."

"Was?"

I let out a shaky breath, and a few more tears blind my vision. "She died in January. Graham and I were supposed to have dinner with her, but he bailed last minute as we were leaving. He had business to go deal with, so I went over myself. She was already gone when I got there." Burying my face in my hands, I cry softly, the image of my mother dead something I can never erase from my mind, the painful reminder there every single day when I look in the mirror.

"I'm sorry," I mumble, mopping at my face with a fresh tissue.

"There is nothing to apologize for," Dr. Klein tells me gently, a sad smile on her face. "This is why you're here, Sadie, to talk about what you're feeling. I'm here to listen."

"Thank you." I take a deep breath, calming myself down.

"You're welcome. It sounds like it's been a hard year, but also a long time coming."

"Yeah. I guess the real reason I'm here is I want to start reclaiming my life. Moving here has changed everything, and I want to be able to have real relationships. But every time I start opening up to people, letting myself go, I clam up. I start retreating into myself."

"And why do you think that is?"

"I don't trust anyone," I state, sitting up straight, determined not to hide anything. I know this is a place where I'm totally safe, so I can speak truthfully. "I know it's not fair to say that, but it's true. I guess I trust people as well as I can, but I want to be able to completely. I want to have friends, a good life. And I'm afraid I won't be able to."

Dr. Klein sets her notebook on the table in front of us and leans forward on her knees, reaching out to squeeze my hand. "Can I ask you something?"

I nod. "Of course."

"You told me you were referred to me by someone you knew, someone who wants to help you start your life over, correct?"

Carmen's smile appears in my head, images of our girls' night last week standing out in my head. "Yeah."

"Sounds to me like you've already made a friend, Sadie. Now you just need to work on believing that you deserve these things."

Biting my bottom lip, I nod at her again, in full agreement. And when I leave her office thirty minutes later, I feel the boulder lying across my shoulders slowly starting to inch its way off. I know I have plenty of work to do, and a ways to go, but Dr. Klein is right.

It's time to start believing in people. Myself especially.

CHAPTER TEN

GARRET

"S HUT UP, B RODY. M Y DANCE MOVES DID NOT SCARE her off." I slap my brother on the back of his head, but he just chuckles and skirts around the kitchen island. Hanging out at my place after a work shift, I'm trying to get Brody's opinion on what I did wrong with Nacole, but the fucker can't stop giving me shit. He's about to get his ass kicked if he doesn't watch it.

"Chill out, bro. I'm just messing with you. Don't get your panties in a twist."

"Brody…."

"But really, man. Two weeks since the concert and you've barely spoken to her. Yep, definitely your dance moves. Fo sho." Brody ducks when I take a swing at his head and laughs again, stepping onto my back porch with a beer in hand. Groaning, I grab my own and head out after him.

"What are you, fucking fifteen? And who the hell even says 'fo sho' anymore?"

"Your amazing brother does, obviously." He folds over in a bow and I roll my eyes.

"Well, amazing brother, tell me. How awesome would it have felt if Lindsey stiffed you the first time y'all went out?"

Brody's eyes narrow at me as he takes a pull from the bottle. "Screw off, man."

"Exactly. It would've sucked. So either shut the hell up or help me, because at this point, I'm ready to throw her a bone and get down on my knees."

Brody chokes on his beer with laughter, and I think back on my words. "Oh, for fuck's sake, man. Grow the fuck up."

Turning on my heel, I go back inside while I finish my beer, heading right for the fridge to grab another. When I shut the door, my brother is behind me.

"Sorry. I'm being a dick, and that's not fair. I had to fight for Linds, in more than one way, and I can't imagine her not being by my side. I'm sorry. I wish I could help, or had some insight into Nacole, but if I'm being honest, even though she's worked for me the past couple months, I know boo about her."

"Yeah, I know, man. I just don't get what happened. I like her, and I thought maybe we could've been good together. I've spent the last decade on my career, working my ass off to make something of myself, and now I'm a month away from the detective's exam. I don't know. Maybe I'm pathetic, but I really like her."

"So call her. Pretty simple thing to do, if you ask me."

"Yeah, maybe. Now let's go fire up the Xbox so I can kick your ass in *Call of Duty*."

Brody finishes his beer and drops it in the trash. "You're on."

I follow him into the living room, his words ringing loudly in my head. I've spent weeks just letting her slip through my fingers, not that I have any control over it. If she doesn't like me, she doesn't. I'm a thirty-three-year-old man, not a teenager who can't handle rejection. But I also need to grow a set and find out once and for all.

§

"Nashville PD. Open up!" Slamming my fist against the door, I lean toward it, trying to hear any commotion inside. Jace stands next to me, trying to look in one of the windows. We received the call only a few minutes ago for a reported domestic disturbance, but the apartment is silent, and nobody is answering.

"What do you think?" Jace asks, and I shrug, leaning my ear against the door. The sound of something crashing perks us both up, and I resume my pounding on the door. A woman cries out, and I jump into action. Stepping back, I don't waste a second before I kick the door in, the thin wood cracking open easily. Keeping a hand on top of my secured gun, I head straight for the commotion, shouting to announce our presence.

A young man is in the tiny kitchen, his hand wrapped around a woman's neck, her face littered with cuts and bruises. Jace shoves past and grabs him, wrestling him down to the ground. Helping the woman out of the area, I radio for them to roll an ambulance and have her sit on the couch. She's crying and frantically trying to pull her ripped shirt over her body.

"Ma'am, I'm Officer Walker. What's your name?"

"I'm… I'm Alison Grady."

"Miss Grady, can you tell me what happened?"

She looks over her shoulder as Jace hauls the man from the apartment, reading him his rights as they go.

"He's my boyfriend, Lance. I don't know why he was so mad." She buries her face in her hands and I gently pat her on the shoulder as I kneel in front of her. She tearfully gives me the rest of her statement, and I fight not to blow my cool the entire while. I hate nothing more than pieces of shit who beat on women. Scum of the earth. I'm glad Jace got to him first.

The paramedics arrive a few minutes later, and I step aside while they check her out. Helping her out to the ambulance, I tell her Jace and I will be by later to check on her. With a tearful smile, she reaches up and hugs me hard.

"Thank you," she whispers.

"Only doing my job, ma'am."

Tucking my notepad in my pocket, I head over to the squad car where Jace is waiting, the piece of shit cuffed in the back seat.

"She okay?" Jace asks, and I shrug, tapping the roof of the car.

"She will be. Let's get him to the station."

"Roger that."

Moving around the hood of the car, I climb into the passenger side and Jace cranks the engine. The ambulance pulls out ahead of us and we make the drive downtown in silence.

When we arrive fifteen minutes later, Jace goes around back and grabs the perp, leading him inside. I follow after, and as I'm stepping into the bullpen, my phone vibrates with a text.

Nacole: Hey. Are you busy this weekend?

Garret: Well hey, stranger.

Nacole: Sorry, been super busy with work.

Garret: I'm supposed to help my dad this weekend. Why?

Nacole: Well, I have some free time and I was hoping we could talk.

Garret: I'm free tonight.

Nacole: I can't.

Garret: Big plans.

Nacole: Garret, this weekend. I need to go.

Garret: Fine.

Locking my phone, I shove it back in my pocket and

head over to my desk, mulling over the last thirty seconds. Nacole seemed testy in those messages, and if she needs to talk to me so badly, why can't she do it tonight? I've been strung along since before the concert. Or have I?

Maybe she really only wanted to be friends all along. Maybe I pushed her.

Fuck.

I don't care. I'm done waiting around for her to keep doing circles around me. I need answers, and I sure as fuck am not waiting four days. No, we're talking.

Tonight.

Decision made, I begin the necessary paperwork for the arrest, making a note to let Jace know I told the woman that we would check in on her later tonight. Blowing out a deep breath, I focus on the job at hand. And knowing that tonight I'll hopefully have the answers I need, I find it easy to get it done.

§

"Hey, bro, got a quick question?" Climbing into my Jeep, I tuck my phone against my ear as I talk to my brother.

"What's up, man?" Brody asks. I can hear the loud noise of the bar in the background.

"Is she working tonight?"

"Who, Linds? Nah, she's on shift at—"

"Brody…."

"Chill, Garret. No, Nacole isn't working tonight.

Requested the rest of the week off, as a matter of fact. Why?"

"No reason. Thanks, little bro."

"Go get her, tiger."

Tossing my phone in the cup holder, I crank the engine, laughing when Blake Shelton blasts through the radio. I take off, heading for Nacole's place. I know I should call her first, but I don't want to give her an opportunity to run from me.

The drive doesn't take long, and before I know it, I'm turning into her driveway. Killing the ignition, I pull the keys out and climb down from my vehicle.

Shoving my keys in my pocket, I stride up her walkway and onto her front porch. Taking a deep breath, I reach out and push the doorbell, my hands in my back pockets as I rock on my heels. After a few moments, I reach out to knock on the door when it's yanked open, revealing a shocked and disheveled Nacole.

"Garret?"

Her eyes and nose are red, hair down in a tangled mess. She looks like she's been crying, and when she folds her arms over her chest, I see a tissue in one of her hands.

"Hey, Brody said you weren't working tonight, and you said you wanted to talk."

"I said this weekend, Garret. I told you no for tonight. What do you want from me?" Her voice is shaky. I motion to come inside, and without looking me in the eye, she waves me in, huffing out a breath in annoyance.

"I'm sorry, but you've just been so distant lately, and

I've been worried about you."

"Well, clearly I'm fine."

"Yeah, you look wonderful," I snap, and her eyes widen, filling with tears at the harshness of my voice. She drops her head and buries her face in her hands, shoulders shaking while she cries. I'm half tempted to search the room for cameras, someone waiting to shout, "Gotcha!"

"Nacole—"

"Please, Garret. Just leave me be. Today isn't a good day."

"Yeah, sorry to say, but that isn't happening. There is no way I'm leaving you this upset. Please talk to me. I hate seeing you like this."

Nacole takes a couple deep breaths and wipes her tears, trying to get control of herself. My hands itch to reach out and hold her, but she doesn't seem to want that.

"Today is my mom's birthday."

"Okay."

"She died in January. This is her first one since."

"Shit."

Nacole tries to put on a brave face, but I can see the pain etched in every muscle. Tears cascade down her cheeks as her bottom lip trembles.

"Come here," I say, holding my arms out, and she walks straight into my embrace, face buried in my sweatshirt as she cries. "I'm so sorry, sweetheart," I mumble, pressing a kiss to the top of her head.

"I miss her so much," she whispers.

I walk us backward until we sit on the couch, and she turns so she can wrap her arms around my neck. Rubbing my hands up and down her back, I gently run my fingers through her soft hair. After a few minutes, I pull back and brush her tears away, placing a soft kiss to her forehead.

"Here's what we're gonna do, okay?"

Nacole gives me a questioning look, and I give her a small smile.

"I'm gonna go in the kitchen and make you something for dinner. Then you're gonna tell me all about your beautiful mother, and you can either cry or not cry, but I'm gonna be here for you no matter what, okay?"

"How do you know my mom was beautiful?"

"Do you look like her?" I ask.

"Yeah, I look almost exactly like her."

"Then that makes her the second most beautiful woman in the entire world. Only second to her daughter, that is."

Nacole bites her bottom lip and then nods, eyes shining with unshed tears. "Thank you, Garret."

"Of course. I'm always here."

Squeezing her hand, I stand from the couch and head into her kitchen, searching the cabinets to find something to make for dinner. I'm pulling a box of pancake mix from the cabinet when I turn and find her standing in the doorway, a small smile on her face. Giving her a wink, I turn back around and busy myself with taking care of my girl.

Wait. My girl?

Shit. I'm screwed.

CHAPTER ELEVEN

NACOLE

"So, tell me something about yourself. Now that I've snotted on you and you made me these delicious pancakes, I feel like I need to know something." Stuffing the last bite of my meal in my mouth, I smile at Garret over my small kitchen table.

"Well, what do you want to know?" His blue eyes bore into mine and my heart races. Today is a hard day for me, but Garret is making it better. And so much easier.

"Well, you never did tell me how old you are."

"Thirty-three."

"Old man," I joke, laughing when he tosses a wadded-up napkin at me.

"Oh yeah? And how old you are?"

"Twenty-nine."

"Pshh. You're old as hell too. Pushing thirty? Damn, better get you a wheelchair. Wouldn't want you to break a hip."

"Oh shut up," I growl, hopping up from my chair and bringing my plate to the sink. While Garret hurries to come after me, I open the container of Cool Whip and grab a freezing cold handful. I spin around and he's standing behind me, arms reaching out for me, clearly worried he hurt my feelings. I take advantage, taking two steps before giving him a face full of Cool Whip.

The look on his face sends me into a fit of giggles, his bright eyes wide behind the white cream. Swiping a hand across his face, he wipes most of the mess off, except for a few streaks on his forehead and cheek. A wicked gleam comes to his eyes, and I have no chance to react before I'm in his arms. He kisses me hard, the taste of the sweet cream and his own a combination to die for, his arms strong around my waist.

Garret devours my mouth in a kiss that sets my body on fire and has goose bumps prickling my skin. He tangles a hand in my hair and gently pulls it, tipping my head back so my bare neck is exposed to him. His scruff rubs against the column of my neck as he presses soft kisses to it, causing me to shiver.

His eyes meet mine, looking for me to grant him permission to continue. Reaching behind us, I grab a hand towel and wipe his face until there's no Cool Whip left anywhere. Up on tiptoes, I kiss him again, threading my fingers behind his neck. Lifting me gently, he sets me on the counter and settles himself between my legs, his arms on the countertop.

"What are we doing?" he whispers, and I hide my face

in his neck.

"I don't know," I mumble, and it's the truth. I'm certainly not ready to be intimate with him, no matter how badly my body reacts to his touch. How much I crave his touch everywhere.

"Just talk to me. Tell me what's going through that pretty head." Garret drops his lips to my shoulder, and I tilt my head to the side, wanting him to move my tank top and continue what he's doing.

"I like you a lot, Garret."

"I couldn't tell," he jokes.

"Be serious," I groan.

He chuckles against my skin, then lifts his head, looking me right in the eyes. I take in everything I see— the laugh lines around his eyes, the way his full bottom lip looks with his white teeth biting into it. His dark hair longer since I last saw him, curling everywhere in the most incredibly sexy way.

"I am though. I can tell you're hesitant to start anything with me, and while I don't know why that is, I respect it. But you run so hot and cold with me, Nacole. I know I'm this tough cop, but I do have feelings buried somewhere under this glorious chest."

I drop my head back and laugh hard, Garret shaking his head at me.

"Wanna tell me what's so funny, you goof?"

"Nothing, just laughing about your chest comment."

"I speak nothing but the truth."

"Yeah, well we'll see. But for real, Garret? I'm sorry

for how I've been. My past isn't exactly pretty, and one day I want to tell you about it. I'm working on it. One day at a time. So for now? Well, I think I'm ready to see where this could go. I want to take things slow though, if you're okay with that?"

Garret smiles. "You're telling me I finally get to take you out on a real date? Yeah, I'm really fucking good with slow, sweetheart. Whatever you want. As long as we go slow together."

"Deal," I whisper, then lean forward, placing my lips to his. This day started out as the second worst day of my life, but since Garret got here, it's been better. We've talked about Mom, and I told him all kinds of stories of me as a teenager.

But this moment, right here?

This is the one I'll be telling for years.

When my broken heart finally started to heal.

§

"Hi, I'm Nacole, and I'll be taking care of you all tonight. Can I start you with some drinks?"

The small group of patrons orders a pitcher of Bud and the appetizer sampler, and I head back to the kitchen to place the order before grabbing their beer.

Brody gives me a smile as he hands it over, and I take it from him with a raised brow.

"What?" I ask.

"Nothing. Glad you and my jackass brother got your

heads on straight."

Rolling my eyes, I can't help laughing at him as I carry the pitcher to the table, placing it down in the center. After asking if they need anything else, I head back over to the side of the bar, all my tables okay for the moment.

Hearing the bell jingle at the door, I look up to see Hunter and Carmen walk inside hand in hand. Carmen rushes over when she sees me, throwing her arms around me in a tight hug.

"Hey, girl," she greets.

"Hey, glad you guys came in. Hi, Hunter," I direct behind her, her husband standing with his hands on her shoulders.

"Hey, Nacole, great to see you again." Stepping around Carmen, he gives me a gentle hug, and for the first time in a long time, I don't inwardly freak out over a man touching me. Hunter leans over to press a kiss to Carmen's head, then turns to go over to the bar, reaching across it to clap Brody on the shoulder.

"How are you?" she asks me quietly, and I know what she's really asking. It's been about two and a half weeks since she gave me Dr. Klein's phone number, and I haven't really had a chance to talk to her. Looking at the large clock on the wall, I see it's only a few minutes until I'm supposed to take my break.

"Give me two seconds," I say, walking around her to the bar. "Hey, Brody, can I take my break a little early?" I ask, motioning toward Carmen.

"Go for it."

"Thank you."

Pulling off my apron, I toss it over the bar and go back to Carmen, grabbing her hand so I can drag her out back to the ladies' room. Shutting the door behind us, I lean against it.

"I never got a chance to thank you, so thank you. Seriously, Carmen. Dr. Klein is incredible."

She smiles at me. "She really is. I still see her once a month, you know."

"Really?"

"Yeah. Not so much to talk about Craig, just more to visit and see her. She's just... good for the soul, you know?"

"I know exactly what you mean."

"So, have you talked to Garret yet?"

My cheeks darken and I look away, Carmen's giggle causing a smile to grace my heated cheeks. "Yeah, he came over the other day and we talked. It was Mom's birthday."

Carmen's expression saddens, and she gives me another hug. "Oh, girl, I'm so sorry."

"It's okay. And it really is. I had told him I wanted to talk this weekend, but he just showed up. I couldn't exactly keep it together when he did, and we spent the entire afternoon and night together. Told him about her, showed him the few photos I have. It was... it was really nice. I mean sure, it was the worst day, but he made it better."

"I'm so happy for you."

"I told him I was ready to see where this would go.

I've seen Dr. Klein five more times since our first visit, and she thinks I'm ready too. I told Garret I wanted to do slow, but I'm ready. I also think I'm ready for another big step too. But I want his help, and in order to do that, I have to confide in him."

"About what?"

"I want to file for divorce. And I want to submit all the evidence of his abuse."

"Holy shit, Nacole. I'm so proud of you."

"Sadie," I tell her, and she raises an eyebrow at me.

"Huh?"

"Shit, I really should be telling Garret this first. Whatever. My full name is Sadie Nacole. When I moved here, I decided to use my middle name, mostly to try and separate myself from my old life. From Graham. Nacole is my mom's name."

"Your secret is safe with me, I promise. But you need to tell him that. And all of it. I think you'd be surprised how well he'd take it. Though I guess I shouldn't say 'well,' because if he reacts the way Hunter did, you'll be bailing him out of jail. But supportive is the key word."

"Yeah. And I'm going to. When the time is right."

Carmen steps forward and places her hands on my shoulders, squeezing gently. "Trust me. The time will always be right. Garret is a good man, and one hell of a cop. And he cares about you. No matter when you tell him, he'll understand. I truly believe that."

We make small talk for a few more minutes before we head back out, my break over and Carmen heading back to Hunter. When she sits next to him, he turns over his shoulder to give me a wink, and I know she's right. If Garret is even one-tenth the man that her husband is, I have absolutely nothing to worry about.

§

Clicking away on my keyboard, I hit Purchase and do a little dance, so excited that I got them. I've been trying to come up with the perfect idea for our first official date. I told Garret that I wanted to surprise him, and when I found the tickets, I just knew I had to grab them. And they weren't too pricey, so even better. When I get the email notification on my phone a few minutes later, I do another little jive, knowing I look totally ridiculous.

Thank you for your purchase.

Confirmation number for 2 General Admission tickets to Luke Bryan.

I mean, maybe I picked Luke Bryan because who doesn't love him, but I know for a fact that Garret's just as big a country fan as I am, so I can't wait to surprise him.

Closing the email, I pull up my text messages and scroll to my chat with Garret. I know he's working right now, but it can't hurt to tease him just a little.

Nacole: Hey you. I have a surprise for you.

Garret: Oh yeah?

Nacole: Yes, sir. Don't make plans for Saturday at 7.

Garret: Jesus, woman. Don't call me sir. You have no idea what that does to me.

Nacole: My bad ;)

Garret: I look forward to it. Please tell me it involves me doing dirty things to your sinful little body.

My cheeks turn bright red and I clench my thighs together. *Fuck.*

Nacole: Nope. But it does involve you and me. Doing something.

Garret: Just got a call. I'll talk to you tonight.

Nacole: Be safe.

Garret: Always.

Smiling, I lock my phone screen and toss it on the couch, needing to get showered before I head out and run some errands.

Saturday can't get here soon enough.

CHAPTER TWELVE

GARRET

Shoving my stuff into my duffel bag, I sling it over my shoulder and head out into the bullpen. My shift ended about twenty minutes ago, and now I'm headed to my parents' to help my dad with a few chores. I haven't been able to get a peep out of Nacole as to what her plan is for tomorrow, but she's really excited, so I can't help feeling the same.

Finding Jace on my way out, I bump my fist against his.

"Have fun tomorrow night, man."

"I'll text you."

Strolling out to my Jeep, I toss the duffel in the back seat and climb in. After sending a quick text to my dad letting him know I'm on my way, I head out, the local radio station cranked. As I make the short drive, my mind wanders to Nacole. I'm not sure what I'm more drawn to, those big brown eyes or her smile. Hell, it would be a lie to say her body doesn't make me hard as stone every time

I see her. She's so beautiful that she takes my breath away, and she has no idea. Nacole is a rare beauty, and I plan on doing everything in my power to show her just how much she is.

Pulling in my parents' driveway ten minutes later, I park alongside my mom's Nissan and hop down, finding her in the front garden tending to the flowers she loves so much.

"Is that the prettiest lady in all of Tennessee in front of me?" I greet, shoving my hands into my front pockets.

Mom brushes her pants off and pulls off her gloves, covered in soil.

"Nope, but it is the biggest kiss ass in all of Nashville coming to visit me," she teases, and I reach down to hug her tight, rocking her back and forth.

"Damn straight," I tell her, pulling away to kiss her cheek.

"Your father's already started, honey. He's out back."

"On my way." Jogging around the side of the house, I find Dad standing just below the deck, loading wood along the side of the house. There are a couple axes stuck in a stump and piles of wood everywhere, just waiting to be cut and stacked.

"'Bout time you got here, son."

"I'm ten minutes early, Dad."

"Just busting your chops. Let's get started. The sooner we finish, the sooner your mother can make us something to eat."

Chuckling, I grab an axe and head over to a pile,

picking up a log as I go. In one swing, I split it in half and look at my father.

"Still only doing chores so Momma will cook for you, I see?"

"Garret, if you find a woman who can cook even half as decent as that woman, then you keep a hold of her. Best thing about her is she knows the way to my heart, and she loves doing it. Probably why these pesky fifteen pounds won't go anywhere."

"Fifteen, huh?"

Dad laughs. "I'm carrying my own food baby, but it's been nine months and this fucker just ain't ready to leave."

Roaring with laughter, I split the log again, Dad coming alongside me to grab his own axe. We take turns until we have more split wood than logs. Dripping in sweat, I swipe my forearm over my forehead and drop the axe, getting busy stacking the wood against the house.

The sun has just started to set when we finish. Mom yells to us from the deck, and I tell Dad I'll be right in. Swinging over to my Jeep, I grab the spare T-shirt I brought and strip off my sweaty shirt, using it to wipe my face.

I'm pulling the clean shirt on when my phone starts ringing from my pocket. Yanking the shirt down, I dig my phone out and see it's Nacole calling me.

"Well, hey there, beautiful."

"Hey. So, I know you're busy at your parents', and I don't wanna keep you from them, but I have just a quick favor."

"You name it." Heading back to the house, I take my time walking so we don't have to end the call yet.

"What time do you think you'll be leaving tonight?"

"Not sure. Probably in the next hour or so. Why?" She lets out a loud sigh and I begin to worry. "Everything okay?"

"Yeah. I'm just getting home from work and my whole kitchen is flooded. I left the dishwasher running when I left earlier today and I don't know what happened."

She sounds close to tears, so I stop walking and check my watch, unsure of what I should do. I want to help her, but I also don't want to go running out on my mom when she's been cooking all day either.

It takes me a minute, but I have an idea. Nacole only lives a few minutes away, so it should work.

"Did you get the water shut off yet?" I ask, stepping onto my parents' porch.

"Yeah, and I've got towels everywhere, but I don't know what else I can do."

"Get changed. I'll be there in ten minutes."

"No, Garret, I don't—"

"See you soon."

Ending the call without letting her get another word in, I rush inside, finding both my parents in the kitchen, Mom stirring something on the stove.

"So, would you mind if I go get a guest for dinner?"

Mom spins around with a giant shit-eating grin on her face and I shake my head, rubbing a hand over the back of my neck.

"Is it the young lady you told us about, the one who works at Brody's bar?"

"Yeah, it is. We're trying to figure things out and take it slow. She called me just a minute ago. Her kitchen is all flooded and she sounded upset, so I thought maybe it would cheer her up."

"Just like your father," my mom laughs. "Go get her, sweetheart. Dinner can wait a little bit longer, and we have more than enough to go around."

"You're the best." Kissing her cheek, I turn and rush back outside, hurrying to my Jeep. In seconds I'm pulling onto the road, heading toward Nacole's place.

When I turn into her driveway a little bit later, I don't even bother shutting off the vehicle. Hurrying to her front door, I rap my knuckles on it and she swings the door open, dressed in a simple white T-shirt and loose jeans, her long dark hair flowing down her back.

"Let's go," I say, reaching for her hand.

"Wait, what?"

"You're coming with me to dinner at my parents.'"

"No way, Garret. Are you out of your mind?"

"Not at all," I chuckle. "Come have dinner with us, and when I drop you off, I'll take a look at your dishwasher, okay?"

"I don't think this is a good idea."

"Why not?"

Nacole runs her hands through her hair, nervously trying to straighten her appearance, but she looks perfect.

"I'm not even your girlfriend, Garret. What will they think of me? I'm not...."

I take a step forward, crowding her space, but only just a little.

"Who cares what you are? So you aren't my girlfriend, but you're the girl I really like, all right? This isn't some 'meet the parents' game. I want you there. Please?"

Her teeth sink into that plump bottom lip and I step even closer, reaching out to gently cup her face, tilting it up toward mine.

"Please," I whisper, and she closes her eyes. I wait patiently, and just when I think she's gonna tell me to get out, her eyes open and they're sparkling.

"Okay, Garret Walker. I'll come to dinner at your parents' house. Happy?"

"You have no idea." Dropping my mouth to hers for a soft kiss, I pull away and place a kiss to the tip of her nose. "Let's go. Mom's been cooking all day, and you're in for a treat."

Stepping inside to grab her purse, she locks the door behind us and we walk hand in hand to my still-running Jeep. Helping her into the passenger side, I close the door behind her, then jog around the hood and climb in, looking over to see her buckling in.

"By the way, you look fucking beautiful," I say, and without another word I drive us to my parents'. Halfway there, I reach out for her hand, and my heart warms when she lets me hold it the rest of the ride.

§

A couple hours later, we're helping my mom clean up from dinner. Nacole really hit it off with them, and my mom has been beaming the entire time. While the ladies do the dishes together, my dad grabs me and pulls me into the living room.

"You did good, son," he tells me, wrapping his arm around my shoulders.

"Well thanks, but we aren't even really a couple yet. Appreciate it all the same though."

"I saw how she looked at you during dinner, Garret. She likes you, and it's obvious you like her too. I hope it works out."

"You and me both, Pops."

We head back to the kitchen, and Mom grabs a dish out of the fridge and sets it on the table.

"You kids gonna stay for dessert?"

"I'd really love to, Mrs. Walker, but I need to get home so I can figure out what's wrong with my dishwasher. I'm sure Garret can come back after he drives me home."

Nacole looks to me, but I shake my head.

"Can we take some for the road, Momma?"

My mother gives me a knowing smile and hastily dishes apple pie into a large Tupperware container. Snapping the lid on tight, she hands it to Nacole and then pulls her in for a hug, Nacole gripping the container tightly. Mom whispers something in her ear, and I don't miss the emotion that crosses my girl's face.

Saying a quick goodbye to my dad, she whispers that she'll meet me in the car. I look back to my mom with a raised eyebrow.

"She'll be okay, honey. Take her home. I'll call you tomorrow."

"Love you," I tell her, giving her a tight squeeze.

Shaking my dad's hand, I head out after Nacole. She's leaning against the side of my Jeep, the Tupperware container still clutched in her hands.

Striding over to her, I lean my hands on the hood of the vehicle and look down at her, noting a few tears on her cheeks.

"What is it?" I ask softly, brushing a tear away before tucking a strand of hair behind her ear.

She sniffs loudly, but looks at me with a huge smile.

"I love your mom," she says, and I know the tears are evidence of her missing her own mother.

Smirking, I press a chaste kiss to her forehead and then motion to the Jeep.

"Shall we?" I ask, and she nods, going around to hop in. Settling myself behind the wheel, I turn to her before starting the engine. "Thank you for joining us tonight."

"I'm glad I came. Thank you, Garret."

"Anytime." Grabbing her hand, I kiss the back of it and start the engine.

The drive to her house is quiet but for the soft strains of the radio. When we pull up at her house, she undoes her buckle and turns to me.

"I know it's getting late, so you don't have to look at

my kitchen if you don't want."

"I don't mind," I tell her. "I'm off shift tomorrow anyway. We can get it taken care of so my surprise doesn't get ruined for tomorrow, right?"

"We can't have that, mister."

We walk into her house and I find towels strewn all over her kitchen, the cabinets under her sink still wide open.

"Let's see what we got here," I say and crouch in front of the pipes with a flashlight so I can see better. It looks like one of the pipes was overdue to be replaced and cracked, hence the water everywhere.

Looking over my shoulder, I go to ask her for help, but she's nowhere to be found. Shrugging, I set about detaching the pipe. In my head, I do the math and know I'll have just enough time to get to the local hardware store before it closes.

"Hey, Nacole, can you come here a second?"

She pads into the kitchen in a pair of sweatpants and a loose-fitting T-shirt, her long hair pulled up on top of her head.

"What's up?"

"The hardware store closes at nine, so I'm gonna run over there really quick to grab what I need to fix this. You wanna come?"

"No, I'm just gonna hang out here, if that's okay? I wanted to catch up on my favorite show."

"No worries. I should be back in about an hour, okay?"

"Okay, I'll be here."

"Back in a bit." Kissing her cheek, I head out, taking my keys from my pocket as I go.

Pulling into the hardware store parking lot twenty minutes later, I jog inside and look at my watch, seeing I have thirty minutes. After grabbing what I need, I check out.

About thirty minutes later, I'm walking up to Nacole's front door, knocking softly before I enter. She's curled up on the couch under a navy blanket, completely immersed in her show with a small plate on the coffee table containing remnants of my mom's apple pie.

She hits Pause when I walk in. "How'd you do?" she asks, yawning loudly as she gestures to the bags.

"I should be able to get this fixed no problem. Just holler if you need me."

She nods at me and as I'm crossing into the kitchen, I hear her show turn back on.

Sorry, but nothing about dating twenty girls at once sounds at all appealing to me.

I'll stick to just one, thank you.

§

An hour and a half later, I'm putting my tools back into the bag I brought in not long ago. Making sure to turn her water back on, I'm closing the cabinets when I hear the soft sounds of Nacole's voice. Leaving my tool bag on the floor, I cross the kitchen and poke my head into the living room. Sound asleep on the couch, her small body is moving around, tears staining her cheeks.

My heart racing, I hurry over to her and drop to my knees in front of where she lies. She's still asleep, her head thrashing around on the pillow, I reach out to run my thumb down her cheek, soothing her soft skin in circles.

"No, please don't," she whispers, pain etched in her words. My skin prickles and I lean down so my cheek rests against hers, cupping her other one.

"Nacole, wake up, sweetheart. You're okay. I'm right here," I whisper, gently shaking her.

A few moments later, she stops moving around. Slowly, her eyes open and they focus on me. "Garret."

"You okay?" I ask, my thumb still tracing the side of her face.

"Bad dream," she murmurs.

"I figured as much. Anything I can do?"

"I need to just go to bed. I'm exhausted."

She stands up and tosses the blanket onto the couch. I steer her into her bedroom and sit on the edge of the bed, watching her climb in. I stand to go clean up the kitchen when she reaches out for me.

"Will you stay with me?" she asks, her voice quiet in the dark room.

"I need to clean up your kitchen, and then I was gonna leave."

"Please?"

Standing, I move to where she's sitting and reach for the hand she has resting on top of her blanket. Bringing it my lips so I can try and soothe her, I look into her eyes.

"What are you asking me, Nacole?"

She clears her throat and looks up at me through tired eyes. "I'm asking you to stay the night, and I know we're taking it slow, but I want you to stay."

"I don't think—"

"Please, Garret. I don't want to be alone tonight."

Staring down at this beautiful woman, I let out a sigh and smile at her, brushing her hair off her forehead. Kicking my shoes off, I go around to the other side of her bed and climb in, ignoring the discomfort of my jeans. Moving behind her, I rest my hand on her hip. She snuggles back against me, and I bury my face in the crook of her neck.

"Thank you," she whispers, and I kiss her neck.

"You're welcome. Sleep. I'll be here all night, sweetheart."

CHAPTER THIRTEEN

NACOLE

I WAKE UP SLOWLY, THE SUN STREAMING IN THROUGH my open window. I shove the blanket off me and sit up, yawning loudly. Climbing from the bed, I make a quick stop in my bathroom to brush my teeth, then pull my long hair up in a knot on top of my head and go in search of Garret.

Stepping into my kitchen, I find the towels cleaned up and my dishwasher humming lightly. The smell of coffee brings me over to my full coffeepot, a small piece of paper sitting next to it.

Nacole,
Ran home to shower and a grab a couple things.
Be back in a bit.
- G

Smiling, I set the paper back down and reach for a coffee cup, quickly filling it with the fresh brew. Taking a sip, I carry it with me to the bathroom and set it on the vanity while I grab some towels. Taking the fastest shower possible, I emerge from the steam-filled room with my coffee in hand and my long hair up in a fluffy towel, another wrapped around my body. Stepping into my bedroom, I dress in comfortable clothing and pull the towel off my head. Tossing it into the laundry basket, I grab my wide-toothed comb and get rid of the tangles in my hair. Tossing it over one shoulder, I pick up my coffee cup once more and head back to my kitchen.

I'm placing the now-empty cup in the sink when I hear an engine roaring up my driveway. I swear I must be a teenager when the butterflies start up in my stomach, and I can't get rid of the goofy grin on my face. A minute later, a loud knocking comes at my front door.

"Come in!" I yell, rinsing the coffee cup out before turning around to see him enter the kitchen. His dark hair is curling out from below the baseball hat he has on, and his black T-shirt hugs his arms and chest in all the right ways. And don't even get me started on those damn Wranglers. Worn and tight.

When I look up, his blue eyes are filled with laughter, and I know I've been caught.

"Morning," he greets, and I can't help myself. Laughing, I rush over and give him a hug, burying my face in his chest, the smell of his cologne heaven.

"Where'd you go?" I ask, pulling away from him.

He brushes my wet hair off my face, his fingers playing with the strands.

"Went home to shower. Wasn't sure how you'd feel about me using yours, and I didn't want to wake you up to ask."

My eyebrows rise in surprise. "Are you even real?"

Garret starts cracking up, then kisses the top of my head before stepping past me to toss a bag on the counter. "Of course I'm real."

"I don't think you are. You're, like, a book boyfriend come to life."

"A *what?*" He laughs even harder.

"A book boyfriend. You know, the hero in romance novels who's all swoony, and alpha, and kind? He always gets the girl because he's this perfect person who knows all the right things to say and do. He's… I don't know, just the definition of perfect."

Garret crosses his arms over his chest and leans against the kitchen counter. "So, what you're telling me is I'm perfect?"

"Only if you take me out for breakfast," I chide, resting my hands on my hips.

"Now that I can definitely do."

"Good, 'cause I really want waffles. And I want to spend the day with you before your surprise. Do you have anything going on today?"

I almost startle myself with my forwardness, but Dr. Klein said that's important. I need to learn to stand up for myself and tell people what I want; I can't hide behind my insecurities and fears anymore.

"I plan on spending the day with this beautiful girl

I like a hell of a lot. Sound okay to you?" Garret strides forward and loops his arms around my waist, fingers playing with the hem of my shirt.

"Yeah. Let me go get changed, okay?"

"Not going anywhere, Nacole."

Leaving him in the kitchen, I go back into my bathroom to blow-dry my hair. The whole time, I keep replaying his words over and over again. *"Not going anywhere, Nacole."*

Yeah, I'm starting to grasp that concept, Walker. And if it's okay with you, I don't want you to go anywhere. I like you right next to me.

Shit. I'm starting to fall for Garret Walker.

Well that's a wrench in my "go slowly" plans.

Shutting off my hair dryer, I fluff my hair up a little and change into a pair of jeans and a light sweater. It's late summer, but the weather is cooler today, which I kind of enjoy.

Stepping out of my bedroom, I find Garret waiting for me in the living room, kicked back on my sofa.

"Ready to go?"

"Yeah."

Grabbing my purse off the couch, I swing it over my shoulder and walk to the front door, pulling it open. Garret holds it for me and I step out, the morning crisp and sunny.

"Do you want me to drive?" he asks, stepping down from the porch behind me.

"No, I want to. Do you mind?"

Garret shakes his head and follows me over to my car. Unlocking the doors, I toss my purse onto the back seat and find him standing next to me, holding my door open. Shaking my head, I climb in and watch him go around the hood, dropping into the passenger side a second later.

"I'm telling you. Book boyfriend material right there."

"Whatever you say, babe. So tell me something. I'm dying to know. What else does a book boyfriend have?"

Biting down on my bottom lip, I grin at how serious he's taking this.

"Well, they're usually really tall. Muscles galore. A master in the bedroom…." I avoid eye contact when he turns to face me with a huge grin on his face.

"Bedroom master, huh? I could get behind that."

"Oh my God, Garret."

"Shall I throw you down on the bed and then invade your personal space with my—"

"Garret!"

Roaring with laughter, he slaps his knee at his own joke, and I shake my head at this lunatic in the seat next to me. "You are insane," I tell him.

"Hey, you're the one who reads that shit."

"For the record, what I read is romance. And it's beautiful. Corny at times, yes, but nothing is more beautiful than the idea that someone would do anything to protect the woman he loved. Making her feel as if she's the most beautiful person in the world—hell, as if she's the *only* person in his world."

His eyes are trained on me and I force myself to stop,

knowing I'm no longer talking about books. I'm talking about how I wish I could feel. That everything I went through over the last seven years could just be erased, that none of it happened.

It can't, of course. But sitting here in my car, watching Garret laugh over things that Graham never would have, I realize maybe my own world is sitting in the passenger seat of my vehicle, ready to run to the ends of the world for me.

Just maybe.

§

"Are you gonna tell me what we're doing tonight?" Garret winks at me while we stroll hand in hand through downtown. We just left this small mom-and-pop joint to grab a late lunch, then got ice cream after.

"Nope. Not yet."

"Okay, wise guy," Garret jokes, taking a lick of his ice cream cone.

"Tell me about yourself," I say, gripping his hand tight.

"What do you want to know?"

"Anything." And I mean it. I could listen to him talk for hours about nothing and I would still fall under his spell. One he seems to have no idea he has.

"Well let's see. I'm taking the detective's exam in a month," he tells me, and I stop dead in my tracks, looking up at him. "What?" he questions.

"You didn't tell me that!" I exclaim, a huge grin

breaking out on my face.

"It's no big deal," Garret says with a shrug.

"Are you serious right now? That is a *huge* deal."

"Just the next step in my career. I've been thinking about it an awful lot lately, and when the offer presented itself, I jumped. I love my job, and having Jace as a partner is awesome, but I'm ready for more, you know what I mean?"

"Yeah," I tell him, my eyes trailing him up and down. "I know exactly what you mean."

"Being a beat cop is tough shit, and I've seen a lot of things I wish I could erase from my memory. It's hard, and I won't lie to you, Nacole, being with me isn't going to be easy. Especially if I make detective. Long, crazy shifts, no downtime. So I want you to know that now. I think it's the main reason I've never settled down or had a real, honest-to-God, more-than-sex relationship."

Garret steers us toward a small park area with benches all around us. He brings us to the closest one and we sit down, his arm slung over the back of it.

"People think I'm this tough-as-nails badass, and I guess maybe I am, but only when I'm at work. Being a cop has just hardened me to the sadness of the world."

"I'm sorry you go through that." I squeeze his hand and lean my head on his shoulder. "But I'm proud of you, Garret. You've only been in my life a couple of months, but they've been some of the best months of my life, especially since losing Mom. I can never thank you enough for getting me through this week."

"No thanks necessary. Like I said, I'm always here for you."

"I know." Finishing my ice cream, I settle myself more comfortably next to him, and his rough hand moves to rest on my thigh, his thumb rubbing gently. It causes me to shiver, and assuming I'm cold, he pulls me closer.

"Like, take this case we had the other day. Got a call to some run-down apartment building. Domestic disturbance. We figured it would be a typical college student fight, and we'd show up and tell them to knock it off. No, what we found was a man strangling his girlfriend after he'd beaten the holy hell out of her. I wanted to kick his fucking teeth in."

My body stiffens with each word he speaks, but he doesn't seem to notice and continues.

"So I sit her down on the couch to get her statement, and all she could say was that she didn't know why she made him so angry. And all I could think was she had no reason to be asking why. She should've been telling him to fuck off. No excuse for putting your hands on a woman. No matter what."

I nod and force the tears back. This genuinely sweet man is talking about a case at work, but I can't help wondering if he would've been that way with me if I'd called the cops on Graham. If a man like Garret had come rushing in, would I have let him help me?

"But nothing is worse than my first month on the job. Almost beat me. You think you watch shows like *Law and Order* or *Criminal Minds* and be prepared. You're a young twenty-one-year-old, fresh out of the academy, and you can take on this world. Then you answer a 911 call where a three-year-old child has been killed, and at the hands of his own father no less, and your perspective on the world changes."

"Oh my God," I breathe. A few tears break free, and I do nothing to hide them.

Garret wipes them away with his thumb, a look of sadness crossing his face.

"Yeah. Twenty-one and I went home to my mom that night and cried. Like a fucking baby. But then I got up the next day and did my job, and I found that it got better. I got over it. But to this day, I still have a picture in my mind of that little boy, and it'll never go away. That's the reason I want to make detective, because I want to do more than answer 911 calls. I want to be the one who helps put the bastards of the world away. Make it safer so one day when I have children, they'll be safe to live in this world."

We sit in silence for several minutes, my hair blowing around in the breeze. I haven't lifted my head from his shoulder this whole time, and he turns to kiss my forehead.

"Sorry, I didn't mean to unload a ton of shit on you."

"It's okay. I like listening to you."

"Tell Jace that, would you?"

I laugh and he stands from the bench, holding his hand out to me.

"Garret?"

"Yeah?"

"Do you like Luke Bryan?" I ask, unzipping my purse.

"Love his music."

"Good. 'Cause I got us tickets to his show in a few hours."

Garret hooks his thumbs into his belt loops and shakes his head at me, a wry grin on his face. "Woman, what the hell am I gonna do with you?"

"Wouldn't you like to know?" I tease, hopping off the bench. He swoops me into his arms and I laugh, cupping his stubbled cheek.

"I would, actually. We've been dancing around each other for two months, spending every waking moment talking. And the second we're together, the spark ignites. So yes, the second I get to drag you into a bed with me, I don't plan on us leaving unless it's in a wheelchair."

My stomach clenches at his words, and he must know he got me when he winks.

"Trust me, Garret, it's starting to sound better every day. You have no idea."

"Oh, I have an idea, sweetheart. My dick has seen more of my hand in the last couple months than when I was fifteen. He's bored with the one-man show."

"So sorry to hear that," I reply, sticking my tongue out at him.

"You won't be sorry when he's making you arch off the bed and yell my name."

"Holy—"

Garret cuts me off with a fierce kiss, his lips turning

me into a panting, crazy mess. Gentling the kiss, he pulls away and cups my cheeks, his harsh breathing fanning my face.

"You're making me crazy. You said you weren't ready to be with me, and I respect that. But fuck, do I want you."

"What do you want?" I whisper, biting my bottom lip.

His thumb pulls it free from my teeth and rubs back and forth over it.

"I want everything."

And for a minute, it's like we're in our own little bubble. Nobody around us. We're the only two people in the world.

I've felt the connection since I saw him in the bar. I've fought it every day, but I don't want to anymore. I deserve more than my past, and I'm moving forward. And I'm doing it with Garret by my side.

Now I just have to tell him about it and hope he's still next to me at the end.

CHAPTER FOURTEEN

GARRET

W<small>ELL IT'S OFFICIAL</small>.

I, Garret Walker, have officially lost my mind. And it's that tiny brunette who has me wrapped around her finger. The concert last week was kick-ass, and I'm so glad she surprised me with tickets. She knows I'm a sucker for a country music concert, and she used it to her advantage.

Nacole is easily the kindest person I have ever met, and every day she blows me away. I took her out to dinner a couple nights after the concert, and after we paid, she noticed a couple across from us with a newborn baby crying. Clearly they were embarrassed and wanted to get out of there, so on our way out, she grabbed the waiter and paid for their meal.

I have no idea how I got lucky enough to meet her, but I did, and I'm sure as hell not letting go any time soon. The time we spend together has become some of the most incredible moments of my life so far. I'm falling for her, and I just hope to God she is too. I convinced her to come spend a couple days at my place with me, and now I'm only one work shift away from forty-eight hours with my girl. I'm going to romance her ass off.

Yes, I'm charming her. I fucking need her. I won't push her though, and I'll be more than happy to just watch movies and eat takeout and listen to her laugh. But if I have any say in it, I'll finally be claiming her as mine. No more screwing around.

The driver door opening breaks my thoughts, and Jace climbs inside the squad car, offering me a coffee. I accept it gratefully and take a swig, a sickly sweet taste hitting my taste buds.

"Dude," I groan, my mouth turning down at the nasty shit he just gave me. "The fuck is this?"

"That is a pumpkin spice latte, and it tastes like Christmas in a cup."

"Okay, three things," I say, setting the cup in the cup holder. "Christmas doesn't *taste* like anything, because it's not fucking food. Second, it's August, Jace. Stop it. And third, don't make me drink the satanic piss of a pumpkin ever again. I'll fucking handcuff you to the trunk of the squad car and throw pumpkin ass lattes at your head."

"Kinky, man."

"Fuck off. I'll be right back, and that monstrosity better be gone."

Climbing out of the car, I head into Starbucks myself, cursing the existence of my best friend. How in the hell he can drink that shit, I'll never know.

Swinging the door open, I step inside and head over

to the counter.

"What can I get you today?" the young woman asks.

"The opposite of the crap my partner just brought out to me," I grumble, tossing a five onto the counter. "I'll take a black, tall."

It takes her hardly any time to hand it over, and I grab it, telling her to keep the change. Walking back out to the squad care, I climb inside and take a sip of my drink.

"Happy, sunshine?" he retorts, making a scene of drinking both coffees.

"No thanks to your pumpkin-loving ass," I joke, smacking him in the back of the head.

He goes to give me shit back when the radio crackles to life with a call.

"Squad twenty-three on it," I respond, and we pull into the flow of traffic, sirens and lights blaring.

The call we arrive to five minutes later is the usual he-said/she-said bullshit of neighbors who don't like each other. After telling them to go back inside or we'd drag their asses to the station, they shut the hell up and went their separate ways.

The first half of the shift is much of the same, and I soon find myself staring at the clock on the dash, praying time would go faster. At this point, it's not even because of Nacole, it's because the shift sucks.

Not soon enough, it's time to head back to the station to do paperwork, and I couldn't be happier. As we make our way back, my phone buzzes with a text.

Nacole: Do you need me to bring anything tonight?

Garret: Just you.

Nacole: Okay then. But be prepared, I'm not all that exciting on my own.

Garret: Trust me, you are.

Nacole: Do you have condoms?

Choking, I spray water everywhere and cough loudly, trying to get a hold of myself. Jace looks over my shoulder and sees the text mid-cough, and he laughs at me.

Garret: We're covered, don't worry.

Nacole: I figured, just keeping you on your toes. Have a good rest of your shift.

Garret: See you tonight.

Shoving my phone back in my pocket, I look up to see a shit-eating grin on Jace's face. Scoffing, I don't even bother asking him what it's for.

"Damn, love looks good on you, man. Not gonna lie."

"What are you going on about?" I ask, turning to look at him as he parks the cruiser.

"Makes you way less cranky, unless you haven't had your pumpkin spice latte." Climbing from the car, he slams the door shut and I hurry out after him.

"Don't you insult me by talking about that swill," I groan, and he laughs harder.

"Dude, chill. But for real, I'm happy for you, brother."

"Thanks. I think."

Jace jogs inside and I stroll in after him, shaking my head at my dumbass partner. I head toward my desk, but I'm stopped when someone grabs my arm.

"Officer Walker?"

Turning around, I find a young woman with zero makeup, her hair up in a ponytail, and a small smile on her face.

Holy crap.

"Alison?" I ask, and she nods at me.

"Yeah. I was hoping you were here."

"Just got back. Everything okay?"

"Was wondering if you had a minute?"

I gesture toward the bullpen and walk her over to my desk. She sits in the chair in front of it and I sit across from her, leaning my forearms on my desk and holding her stare.

"I just wanted to thank you," she says, and I raise an eyebrow.

"For what?"

"Being so kind that day Lance was arrested. I wasn't in a good place, and you and your partner saved my life."

"Just doing my job," I state, leaning back in my chair.

"No, you guys saved my life. I don't think he was gonna stop that day, and it's because of you guys giving me a chance at a better life that I decided to legally press charges. He's still being held on a hefty bond he can't pay."

"Coward deserves it."

"I moved back in with my parents. My dad flipped his

lid, but they're supportive. I joined a support group, and I'm doing okay."

I smile at her, taking in just how different she is from only a few weeks ago. Alison looks happy and healthy, and the only evidence of that day is a very faint bruise near her jaw. It makes me incredibly happy.

"I'm so happy for you, Alison."

"Thank you, Officer."

"Garret, please."

"Garret. Is your partner around too? I wanted to thank him as well."

"Yeah, Jace should be here somewhere. Let's go find him." I stand to get him when she hugs me again, and this time I hug her back. Not every call ends with a happy tone, and I'm glad to see this one did. When Jace and I went to visit her in the hospital, she told us she was twenty and had only been dating the guy about six months, so I'm glad she got out of that situation. She's way too young to have that much pain in her life.

Jace is over near the vending machines. When he turns around, his reaction is much like mine—shock and happiness. Jace being the kind of guy he is, he leans down and sweeps her into a bear hug, her feet dangling a few inches from the ground. When she leaves the station ten minutes later, her step looks bouncy and we both stand there watching her go.

"Damn," Jace mutters, and I nod. He looks at me with a huge grin and holds up his hand. Bumping my fist against his, I grab him in a half hug. Any shit call today just morphed away. Nothing could bring us down now.

That right there is why I chose this job.

§

Making sure the pot won't boil over, I place the lid on it and check the time. Five o'clock. Nacole should be here soon.

Rushing to the bathroom, I hop in the shower and wash up as fast as I can, stepping out only a few minutes later. Wrapping a towel around my waist, I wipe the steam from the mirror and grab my electric razor, taking my facial hair down to a normal scruff. Giving my hair a quick towel dry, I brush it back off my face and stride into my bedroom to get dressed.

Settling on a pair of worn jeans and a T-shirt, I'm tossing the towel into my hamper when the doorbell rings. Hitting the light switch, I rush downstairs and over to my front door. Yanking it open, I find the most beautiful sight: Nacole standing in front of me, a bag over her shoulder.

"Hi," she greets, and I step out onto my porch to give her a kiss, one of her arms coming around my waist. Pulling away, I usher her inside and take her bag from her, tossing it onto the couch and then turning to look at my girl.

"I am so glad you're here."

"Me too. How was work?"

Taking her by the hand, I lead her over to the couch

and sit down, pulling her down next to me. I recount the events with Alison, emotion crossing her face while I'm telling her.

"That's amazing, Garret. I can't imagine how good that must've felt for you and Jace to see her again. You should be so proud."

"Yeah, not many cases like that end so well. She's so damn young, you know? She deserves to have a great life, not deal with a druggie piece of shit who hurts her like that."

"Well, it's over now." Nacole stands from the couch and walks into the kitchen, her long hair swaying behind her. And damn right I watch that ass as she goes. *Fuck. She's perfection.*

"What's for dinner?" she yells, and I head into the kitchen, finding her at the stove about to lift the lid on the pot.

Stepping up behind her, I place my hands on her waist and rest my chin on her shoulder, kissing her cheek. "My homemade chili."

"It smells delicious."

"You smell better," I groan, and she laughs, turning in my arms to lace hers around my neck.

Taking advantage, I kiss her and back us up until we're next to the wall, her back flat against it. I take advantage and deepen the kiss, the urge to take her against the wall growing stronger when her tongue teases against mine.

I have to force myself to break away, my dick straining against the tight confines of my jeans at her flushed cheeks. She smirks at me, and I have to bite the corner of my cheek. That look on her face is downright sinful.

"How about I give you a tour while dinner is finishing up?" I suggest, and Nacole takes the hint.

I hold out my hand and she takes it, following me throughout the house for the next ten minutes. When we get to my bedroom, she strolls across the room to my bureau, where framed photos sit. She picks up the one of my graduation from the police academy, my parents and Brody standing with me.

"They look so proud of you, Garret."

"Yeah, they are. I've done everything I can to make them too."

Setting the photo down, she picks up another of Brody and me at his wedding. We're both in suits with sunglasses on, and beers in our hands. We took the photo an hour before he got married. I was his best man—greatest privilege I've ever had.

"Garret?"

"What's on your mind, sweetheart?"

She turns to me and lets out a deep breath. "At some point this weekend, I need to talk to you about something really important, okay?"

"Of course."

"I just hope it doesn't make you hate me."

My brow furrows. "Why would you ever think I could hate you?"

"I need you to promise me, okay?"

I sit on my bed and pull her between my legs, her

hands resting on my shoulders. "Nacole, nothing you ever tell me would make me hate you. And I've told you a million times, I'm not going anywhere, okay? You're important to me. So important."

"Okay."

Resting her forehead on mine, she sighs and I pull her even closer to me. Lifting her head, she takes my lips with hers and her small hands cup my jaw, that wicked tongue running along my bottom lip.

Sliding my hands down her back, I groan against her mouth when I finally get my first feel of that ass I love so much. I squeeze and pull her closer to me, and she takes the hint, climbing onto my lap.

Breaking our connection, she looks down at me, panting from the kiss.

"You want to slow down?" I ask, brushing her hair off her face. "We've done things your way from the beginning, and I want you to know we can stop right now, before anything starts."

"I need you, and I'm tired of running from everything. I want to face it head on. And before we do, I really need you to make love to me, Garret. I need you to show me what that really means."

And just like that, my original plans fly out the window.

CHAPTER FIFTEEN

NACOLE

"Sit tight. I'll be right back."

Garret stands with me in his arms and tosses me onto the bed, my hair fanning across the pillows. In a flash he's gone from the room, his footsteps heavy on the stairs. Taking advantage, I strip out of my jeans and shirt, the matching red lace panties and bra the only things left on my body. Making myself more comfortable, I hear him coming back upstairs. My nerves begin to get the best of me, so I close my eyes and pray he's happy with what he sees.

"Fuck."

My eyes fly open to see him in the room, standing stock-still in front of the bed.

"What? Do I not look okay?" Sitting up, I look down at myself in concern.

"Baby, the only way you could look any better is if you didn't have those clothes on."

His words bring a smile to my face, and I bite my lip when he reaches down to adjust himself in his pants. He grabs the collar of his shirt and pulls it over his head, and my mouth drops open. I want to lick every single one of his defined abs, and his broad chest has a light spackling of hair. And don't get me started on that V.

Garret climbs onto the bed, still in his jeans, and makes his way up, settling right on top of me. I spread my legs to make room for him, and he drops his face into my neck.

"You look fucking beautiful. Don't ever doubt for a second that you're the most stunning woman I've ever met. Okay?"

I nod and run my hand down his tight stomach, fingers lightly trailing over his abs. I smile when the muscles bunch, a grimace on his face when I look up. "You okay?"

"Yeah, except my hot-as-fuck girlfriend is lying beneath me in the sexiest fucking things I've ever seen, and she's giggling while touching my damn abs. Yes, I'm fine."

"Girlfriend, huh?"

Garret pushes up onto his elbows and stares down at me, one of his hands twirling a strand of my hair between his fingers.

"I'm about to be inside of you, and I'm quite fond of you, goofball. Yes, you're my girlfriend. Unless you have an issue with that?"

"Nope," I say, popping the P with a grin.

"Good. Now enough of the chitchat. I need to see what you have on." He rises to his knees, his rough hands moving to the thin fabric of my bra and cupping my breasts. They ache for his touch and I squirm around under him, groaning when he chuckles.

"Haven't even gotten to the good stuff yet and you're ready. Gotta say, that's fucking hot, Nacole."

"Garret."

He takes pity on me and moves my legs so they're around his waist as he settles himself between them. He runs a fingertip under the top of my bra and finds my nipple, causing a soft moan to leave my parted lips. Sliding his hands under my back, he unsnaps my bra and lifts it off my body, nostrils flaring when he gets his first view of my bare breasts. And oh hell, when those rough fingers begin pinching and pulling on the sensitive buds.

My back arches against his ministrations, and I try to grind myself against his hips, the ache between my legs growing stronger. Bending over, he takes one of my beaded nipples in his mouth and rolls it around between his teeth, his other hand sliding to the front of my panties.

A finger teases under the band, and I growl in frustration when he doesn't move his hand where I want it. He lifts his head from my breast and looks down at me, his eyelids heavy with lust. Licking his bottom lip, he hooks his fingers into the lacy material and rips them right from my body.

He gives me zero chance to react before he spreads my legs even wider, that wicked fucking mouth dropping right where I need him. The inhuman moan that leaves my lips echoes off the empty walls, and I reach up to grab his headboard. Garret gives me no mercy, attacking my pussy with fervor, holding my hips down with his hands.

"Garret, oh my *God*!"

He growls against me, and the vibrations are almost my undoing. He gives my clit a few teasing licks before taking it between his lips and sucking hard in pulsing motions. My back arches so hard my head barely touches the pillows and I cry out, stomach clenching, my orgasm flying at me with no chance of stopping. It hits me head on and I'm coming, panting hard, his lips riding the wave with me, sending me tumbling into the abyss.

The aftershocks gentle and he lifts his head, wiping his mouth with the back of his hand. My body is coated in a light sheen of sweat, and there's no hiding his rock-hard cock in his jeans anymore. I just had one of the most intense orgasms I've ever experienced, and yet it only intensifies my need for this man.

Sitting up, I kiss him hard, the taste of myself on his lips only spurring me on. Pushing him away, I reach down and undo the button on his jeans, but he moves my hands, climbing off the bed so he can shed them. In just his boxer briefs, he reaches into his nightstand to grab a condom, looking at me as he tears it open.

"You're sure, baby?"

"Uh, yeah. Pretty sure I'm good with all of this, considering what you just did."

He slides his underwear off, and I'm given my first

look at his hard cock. Good Lord. He's not hung like a horse, but it's going to feel fucking magnificent. He's long and thick, and I need him inside me. Now.

Rolling the condom down his shaft, he moves toward the bed and climbs back on, moving so he's sitting with his back against the headboard. My eyebrows rise at him and he grips his cock, moving his fist up and down, eyes filled with lust.

"Get that perfect fucking ass up here, sweetheart. I need to be in you."

Not wasting another second, I do as he says and straddle him. Garret rubs his cock around my clit and my hips jerk, desperate to feel him. I keep my eyes on his as he places himself at my entrance, his hands moving to grip my waist. Slowly, I drop onto him and have to bite my lip to keep from screaming, the pleasure of him stretching my body almost too much, but so fucking good. He groans loudly, and I can't go slowly anymore. We have all weekend for that.

I lift myself off him so only the tip is inside, then lower myself completely so he's fully seated. I gasp and his hands tighten on my hips, fingers biting into my skin.

"Fuck," he grunts, dropping his head to my shoulder.

"What?" I pant, rocking my hips gently, but he stops me. "Come on," I whine.

"You gotta give me a second, babe. Christ, you're so fucking tight."

"It's been a long time," I whisper, and he lifts his head.

"And it's never been like this."

His words hit me hard, and I close my eyes against the tears burning. Burying my face in his neck, I begin to move myself up and down his thick shaft, moaning with every thrust. The angle he's at is rubbing inside of me perfectly, and my legs are shaking already. His hands move to cup my ass and he kneads as we move, his chest sliding against mine.

He never speeds up my movements, just lets me take us on the ride of our lives. He feels impossibly harder inside of me, and his grunts are growing louder. Lifting my head, I take his mouth in a sloppy kiss and our teeth clash, the frantic need building between us. Garret flips us over so I'm on my back and he begins to move.

Hooking my legs around his lean hips, I meet him thrust for thrust, his hips hitting mine harder and faster. Sliding my arms around his waist, I move them up his back, my nails digging into his skin, a growl leaving his mouth.

"Garret…."

"Fuck, you have me so damn close, baby. I need you to come again."

He leans up onto an elbow, his hips not stopping their brutal pace, and slides his hand down to where we're connected, thumb rubbing roughly against my clit. The orgasm I didn't even know was building climbs out of nowhere and my muscles clamp down on him, eyes falling shut as I shake through a climax even more intense than the first.

Garret moves his hand back to the mattress next to my

head and starts to pump even faster, his thrusts forcing the headboard to bang off the wall. In only a handful of strokes, his head falls back on his shoulders and he bites his bottom lip, moaning loudly, his hips locking against mine. Dropping on top of me, he runs his lips up and down my sweaty neck, his body trembling from his own release.

Looking up at him through heavy-lidded eyes, I lick my dry lips.

"Well that was fun. But I think we're gonna have to try a few more times to get the hang of it," I joke, and he laughs, dropping his head to my chest.

"You can bet your sweet ass that we'll be doing lot more of it." My stomach growls loudly, and we both start laughing. "I need to feed you. Come on." Carefully, he pulls out of me and climbs off the bed, going into the bathroom.

"You need to feed me? Who are you, Christian Grey?"

"Who the fuck is Christian Grey? Babe, can you not mention ex-boyfriends when we were fucking having hot-as-hell sex only moments ago?"

Howling with laughter, I look up to find him standing there in a pair of navy sweatpants, not looking quite as amused as I am. Reaching over the side of the bed, I grab the T-shirt he was wearing earlier and pull it on, standing on tiptoes to kiss his cheek.

"Let's go. I'll tell you all about Mr. Grey over a bowl of your chili. I'm starving."

I bounce downstairs and he follows me. Twenty

minutes later, when he realizes just who Christian is, he laughs just as hard as I did the first time.

§

Stepping out of Garret's shower, I look at my reflection in the mirror. I haven't seen this much life on my face in a long time. I run a towel over my wet hair and throw it into a braid, tying it off before going into the bedroom to grab the tank top and sleep shorts I left out. I want to be comfy this weekend, so I don't bother with any makeup or anything fancy. Taking care of the wet towels, I head downstairs to find my boyfriend, the word bringing a smile to my face.

Garret is in the kitchen drinking a cup of coffee, his cell phone pressed to his ear. He looks angry, and I can't tell what's wrong. He drops a kiss to my head and holds up a finger to me, telling me to give him a second. I shrug and go about fixing my coffee. When he ends the call a moment later, he looks at me with frustration.

"Okay, so please don't be mad," he starts, and I roll my eyes.

"What good conversation ever started like that?"

"I need to run into work for just a bit."

"Okay," I say, hopping onto his kitchen counter.

Garret smiles and comes to stand in front of me.

"I'm serious. They need Jace and me to go over some paperwork. There was a glitch in the system, and the reports we handed in yesterday got fucked up."

"Garret, it's fine. I wasn't joking. Honestly. Go do what you need to. I'll be here waiting for you."

"You're too good to me." When he moves to place his coffee on the counter, he knocks my purse to the floor, the contents scattering across the kitchen. "Shit."

I hop down to help him grab everything, and it's then I see my license sitting on the ground. Trying not to draw attention to myself, I scurry to get it, but he grabs it before me. My heart starts racing and I can tell the moment he notices. He stands and turns to me, a puzzled look on his face.

"What's this?" he asks, and he holds it out. "Sadie Nacole Ward" stands out like a giant fucking neon sign and I gulp, unsure of how to begin this conversation.

"It's not what you think," I begin, but anger crosses his face.

"Yeah, 'cause that's a real good fucking conversation starter."

"Garret, please. Let me explain."

"Is this your license?"

"Yes, but—"

"Your name is Sadie?"

I nod, and his eyes narrow. I try desperately to snatch it from his hand, but he holds it out of my reach, not allowing me to touch him.

"Garret—"

"You've been lying to me?"

"Please, just let me—"

"How could you lie to me? I trusted you." His voice

booms through the kitchen and I jump, startled at the harshness to his tone. "Was this some game? Is that all I was, just a joke to you?"

He sounds so hurt and tears begin to fill my eyes, the pain in my heart unbearable.

"Garret, please. Just listen to me. I didn't want to lie to you, I tried so many times to find a way to tell you."

"No you didn't. Because if you had, I wouldn't be finding out now."

"It's not that easy."

"Not that easy? I'm a cop, Nacole. Pretty sure I would've found out eventually. I mean, what else did you lie about?"

"Don't do this, please," I cry loudly, but he doesn't look fazed.

The man in front of me is not the same person I spent the night making love to. Who held me all night. Who whispered how much I had changed his life and how happy he was.

That man is gone, and in his place is the one I've betrayed by not allowing myself to trust him enough with the truth. And the knowledge of that shatters me.

"Don't you dare. Don't you put this on me, Nacole. Don't. I mean, what are you gonna tell me next? That you're married or something?"

"I… I wanted to tell you, Garret. I'm so sorry."

My license falls from his fingertips and the hurt on his face deepens. "You're fucking married? Please tell me you're joking."

I shake my head and he turns away.

"Fuck!" he bellows, slamming his hand against the doorway, the wood rattling beneath his anger.

I close my eyes against his movements, his unexpected reaction scaring me. I know he would never touch me in anger, but right now he's madder than I ever imagined he would be.

"I'm so sorry," I sob, dropping to my knees in the middle of all my stuff.

"You're sorry? I just slept with a married woman, the same woman I've been fucking falling in love with, and you're sorry? I can't even look at you."

He storms from the room and I drop my head to my chest, crying harder than before. He comes back into the room a second later, fully dressed.

"Garret, you promised. Please."

"Yeah, that went out the window the second you fucking lied to me. You *lied*, Nacole. And you broke us in the process. I hope it was worth it."

He storms out the front door, his Jeep starting up a minute later before he goes roaring down his driveway. Left alone, I stand on shaky legs and gather all my stuff. Rushing upstairs, I grab everything I brought and run down the stairs, snatching my purse on the way. I drive home with blurry vision, the tears nonstop.

When I get home, I run inside and slam the door shut behind me. Dropping onto my couch, I curl up and cry, nothing hurting more than my heart. The way he looked at me, the hurt on his face. He'll never forgive me.

An hour or so later, I've finally calmed down, standing in the kitchen pouring myself a cup of tea. Garret hates me, and I don't blame him. But I can't let him think I'm just some cheating whore who ripped out his heart. No, he needs to know the truth.

Placing the streaming cup of tea down, I head into my bedroom closet and grab the cardboard box sitting inside, the contents the most painful moments of my past. Carrying it into the living room, I place it on my coffee table and go in search of a notebook. Finding one in the kitchen drawer, I write Garret a letter. The most honest letter I've ever written.

Taping the note to the top, I slip my feet into a pair of sandals and drive back to Garret's house, praying he isn't there, and praying I don't crash my car. My hands are shaking, and my eyes burn with unshed tears. Even if I've lost him forever, at least he'll know the truth.

He deserves that much. Even if I no longer deserve him.

CHAPTER SIXTEEN

GARRET

Pulling into my driveway, I let out a deep sigh, parking my Jeep in front of my garage. Climbing out, I head inside, mind still racing from earlier. It only took us a few hours to get the paperwork straightened, but I barely paid any attention. I can't decide if I want to just go to bed or drink Nacole out of my thoughts. I mean Sadie. Or maybe it is Nacole. Who fucking knows?

I can't believe I was so blind to her deceit. But as angry as I am, I think the real problem is I hate admitting how badly it hurts, knowing she lied to me.

Knowing we're done.

I wasn't exactly expecting to fall in love with her, but my stupid ass went and did just that. Locking the Jeep, I step onto my porch, a brown box sitting on one of the chairs catching my eye. Grabbing it, I find a white piece of paper taped to the top. Shoving it under my arm, I unlock my front door and carry it inside with me.

Kicking the front door shut behind me, I take the box

into my dining room, dropping it on top of the table and heading back into the kitchen, grabbing a beer from the fridge. Popping the top, I take a pull and drag the box toward me, ripping the piece of paper off it. My name is scrawled across it. Unfolding it, I start reading, knees going weak as I drop into a chair.

Garret,

I have no idea how to say any of this to you, but I need to try, because I owe you that much at least. Please know how badly I wanted to tell you. Every day, I tried to find the strength, but I just couldn't. I didn't want you to look at me in shame or pity. That would've killed me. When I left California, it was to find myself. To find safety. And while I did, I also found you. You have no idea how thankful I will always be for you. Before I met you, Garret, I didn't have any reason to smile or laugh, but because of you, I can. You brought me back to life, and you saved me in ways you'll never understand.

I'm so sorry for lying to you, but even more than that, I'm sorry I hurt you.

I never meant for any of this to happen. But the one thing I'm not sorry about is you. I didn't plan it, but I'm not sorry it happened. Please find it in your heart to forgive me. I want nothing more than for you to be happy. And when you do, I hope you find someone who deserves you. Because I certainly don't. Not after the things I've done.

Be happy, Garret. That's all I want.

Love always,

Sadie

Hands shaking, I toss the paper onto my table, beer

forgotten. Carefully, I pull the top of the box off and find papers and photographs. Lifting the first piece of paper, I see the same handwriting scattered across the lines.

January 13th
Mom has been gone a week. My heart feels like it's broken into pieces. Graham doesn't care. His dinner wasn't done when he walked in the door.
He slapped me twice.
Left a bruise on my cheek. Split lip.

Eyes wide in shock, I notice the photograph under where the paper was. A close-up photo of her face, the purple mark on her cheek, the bleeding cut on her lip.

Holy. Fuck.

Setting them on the table, I reach for the next piece of paper. This time the photo is stapled to the paper at the bottom.

January 18th
I woke up to Graham stumbling home drunk at two in the morning. When I asked him where he'd been, he backhanded me, then told me to make him something to eat. While I was walking downstairs, he told me I wasn't moving fast enough and kicked my feet out from under me.
At three o'clock, I went to the ER for pain meds. Told them I tripped.
Stitches on my jaw. Black eye. Sprained wrist. Sore back.
Came home, and when I told him where I'd been, he laughed at me.
Laughed.

The photo attached has me fighting the urge to vomit. My hand shakes as I hold it up in front of me. My beautiful girl, tearstained and black and blue. I start to reach for the next item in the box, but I can't bring myself to read or look at any more.

Standing from the table, I pace, running a hand over my hair, gripping it tightly to the point of pain. Gritting my teeth, I walk in circles, trying to wrap my mind around this whole thing. But I can't.

Who the fuck would treat someone that way?

"Fuck."

Moving back over to the box, I pull the next piece of paper out. She wanted me to know everything, so as hard as this is, I respect her wishes.

January 31st.

Black eye. Bruises around my throat.

Why? For existing.

I hate my husband with everything in me.

Maybe one day he'll actually kill me. Then the hell I live in will be over and he can't hurt me anymore. Maybe one day.

I don't even realize I'm crying until the tear falls onto the paper. Letting out a broken sob, I drop the paper and reach for the beer bottle, still full. Hurling it with all my strength, it hits the wall with a loud crash, glass and beer flying everywhere. Dropping down into the chair, I hang my head.

Images of her fly through my mind, crying and running, terrified of this man. My heart breaks imagining how scared she must've been all the time. To have written that she wanted to just die. I can't take it.

Then I realize how I acted earlier. I remember the fear in her eyes after I smashed the doorframe, when I shouted at her for lying to me.

I don't even care about that anymore.

Without a second thought, I run out of my house, heading for my Jeep. Jumping inside, I drive blindly to Sadie, tears still blurring my vision.

"Son of a bitch!" I yell, smashing my fist against the steering wheel.

How dare that piece of shit abuse her! He was her husband, for fuck's sake. His job was to protect her.

I'm going between being completely fucking livid with that animal and devastated for her. I don't give a shit if I have to get down on my knees and beg for forgiveness. I just need to get her in my arms, where she's safe.

The normally fifteen-minute drive takes less than ten, and I let out a sigh of relief when I see her car parked in the driveway.

Leaving the engine running, I stumble from my vehicle and race for her front door. I'm only halfway there when she comes walking outside, a black bag in her hands, eyes red and swollen. She stops when she sees me, eyes wide and scared. I walk to her, going slow so as not to scare her. I never want her to fear me, not like that fucking bastard.

"Sadie..."

Her face falls when I speak her real name, her

shoulders shaking with her cries. Stopping when I'm right in front of her, I fall to my knees, hands softly latching onto her hips. Resting my forehead against her stomach, I close my eyes and breathe her in.

"I'm so fucking sorry," I say, tears soaking her shirt when I feel her small arms come around my shoulders as she kneels in front of me. Looking into her eyes, I cup her face, the tears on my face mirroring hers. "Please don't leave, baby."

§

"I just didn't know how to tell you. I was ashamed to admit who I really was."

Lying in her bed together, my fingers trail up and down her back, her forehead pressed to mine. We haven't spoken much, and I'm not sure I'm ready to hear all she's going to tell me.

"I wouldn't have judged you, Sadie."

"I know that now," she whispers, and I shift around so I can look into her eyes.

"How long did this go on?" I ask.

She blows out a deep breath and looks down. "Seven years."

"Jesus," I mutter, pulling her even closer to me.

"Can we not talk right now? Wait...I'm sorry. I have no right to ask you that, and if you'd rather just go home, that's fine too."

"Of course."

Rolling over in the bed, I get comfortable on my back and close my eyes. We got hardly any sleep last night, and after the exhausting start to the morning, I could use a nap. I know I should force myself to stay awake, beg her to tell me everything, but I can't. Sleep takes over my body and I'm vaguely away of Sadie sidling up next to me, her face buried in my neck, and then I'm out.

I'm jolted awake by the sound of a loud ringing. Squinting my eyes open, I realize it's my cell phone on the end table. Checking the display, I answer the call.

"Hey, Brody," I greet, scrubbing a hand over my face.

"Hey. Are you with Nacole?" I fight the urge to correct him, knowing it's not my job to do so.

"Yeah, why?"

"Linds wanted me to call and see if y'all wanted to come out to dinner with us tonight. Nate has the closing shift, and we're heading to that new steak house downtown."

"I appreciate the offer, man, but we're gonna have to pass."

"Can't get outta bed, huh? I feel that."

I scoff and shake my head. "No, we're out of bed. But tonight's not a good night."

"Everything all right?"

Looking over at the empty space next to me, I sigh and lie back on the bed, the phone pressed tight to my ear.

"I'm not sure, bro."

"You know where to find me if you need anything,

Garret."

"Thanks."

"Anytime. I'll text you later."

"See ya."

Ending the call, I drop my phone onto the bed and run my hands down my face. The smell of something delicious takes over my senses, and I climb from the bed in search of its source.

Stepping into the small kitchen, I find Sadie pulling something from the oven before setting it on the stove top. Leaning against the doorframe, I watch her work in silence until she turns around, jumping with a shriek. Laughing, I stride forward and check out what she made.

"Apple pie? Shit, that smells good."

"It was my mom's recipe. I just felt like being close to her today."

"Where are the plates?"

She laughs and swats at my chest. "You know where everything is. There might even be some vanilla ice cream in the freezer."

"Woman, don't play with me," I joke, stepping around her to the freezer. Grabbing the half-gallon out, I carry it over to her small kitchen table, setting it in the center.

"You know this is burning hot, right?"

"Yep. Don't care. You bake things that smell that good and I'll risk the third-degree burns."

Shaking her head, Sadie cuts a slice and carries it over to me. Sitting down, I reach for the plate when she leans over and places a gentle kiss to my cheek. I'm not entirely sure why, but it warms my heart and I grab her by the waist, pulling her onto my lap.

"You don't need to be trying to butter me up, sweetheart. I'm still angry, but you have to know I'm not here out of pity. I'm here because you're my girl. I just wish you'd told me sooner." She nods and I kiss her forehead. Those beautiful brown eyes fill with tears, and I wrap my arms tight around her waist. "Please don't cry," I whisper.

"I can't help it. I told myself every single day to tell you. I knew how wrong it was to lie, but I didn't exactly move here looking for you. I didn't want a new life. I just wanted to be free."

Her words strike a chord with me, and I kiss the corner of her mouth.

"If it makes you feel better, you look more like a Sadie than a Nacole," I joke, and she bursts out laughing, tears running down her cheeks.

Wiping her face, she climbs off my lap and goes over to the sink to clean up, then starts a pot of coffee. I eat in silence, groaning out loud at how good it is. Soon the smell of the rich coffee mingles with the pie, and the aromas are heaven.

Finishing my food, I carry the plate to the sink and wash it, setting it in the strainer. "There any leftover coffee?"

"Yeah, help yourself. And then can you come in here?" I didn't even realize Sadie had left the room until her voice sounds from her bedroom.

"Be there in a second, babe."

Pouring a mug of black coffee, I pad back into her bedroom. She's cross-legged in the middle of the bed, a mug in her hands.

"Sit," she says, pointing to the end of the bed. Raising an eyebrow, I do as she says, folding my legs up under me. We sit in silence for a few minutes, and then she begins speaking.

"I met Graham when I was a junior in college. We had the same business class and we clicked. We became official a couple days later, and we married three months after we graduated. I had plans to open my own business, and he went into real estate. We were married a month the first time he hit me. I had planned dinner out, and he didn't want to go anywhere."

She pauses to take a sip of coffee, and I notice she's avoiding my eyes. I hate it, but I understand. She's having to relive horrific moments, and as much as I hate hearing it, I know she needs to tell me.

"He backhanded me across the face, and I vowed to leave him that night. But when I went upstairs to pack a bag, he was frantic and got down on his knees, begging and pleading with me not to leave him. He was sorry and it would never happen again. Said he was just stressed out from work and the housing market being shit. He was scared that he couldn't provide for me. I offered to start looking into space for a business, told him maybe it was the time for me to start it up."

"What kind of business did you want?" I ask, and a

huge grin covers her face.

"Back then? I wanted to own a clothing shop. But where we lived in California, it would've been too competitive, and Graham didn't want to waste money on a potential."

"Asshole."

"Yeah. Well anyway, I became the doting wife, making sure dinner was always ready, cleaning his laundry, being at his beck and call at all times. My only saving grace was Mom. I saw her at least once a week, and even though he hated going, he knew if he didn't, my mom would start to suspect there were problems. He forced himself through dinners and birthdays, but he always made sure he told me over and over again how much he hated it. Asked why my mom couldn't just find her own friends."

Setting her half-full cup on the end table, she pulls her knees up to her chest and wraps her arms around them. I can't help reaching out to cover her hands with one of my own.

"I was with him for nine years, Garret. I gave him my virginity, all of my trust, and all of me. He shattered it. After Mom died, he became so much worse, like he knew there was nobody else to find out. He could be as cruel as he really wanted and nobody would care."

Sadie uses her arm to brush her tears away, and I lean over to place my coffee cup next to hers. When I sit back down, I pull her legs flush with me so I can hold onto her.

"Take your time, sweetheart. You don't need to tell me everything right now."

"Yes I do. I lied to you for almost three months. I can't forgive myself for that, so I need you to know why. I need you to forgive me."

"Sadie, stop." Pulling her onto my lap, I cup her cheeks, our faces only inches apart. "I do forgive you. You don't need to force it out just so I understand. I read the papers, saw the photos. I understand. And it was not your fault."

"Garret."

"No, you need to really hear me, baby. You didn't do anything wrong. Yes, I'm pissed you lied to me. That fucking hurt. But what hurts more is why. Why you had to lie about anything. There is absolutely no excuse for what he did. None at all. Assholes like him don't even deserve to be called a man. He's a fucking walking piece of shit, and I would love nothing more than to throw him in jail myself."

Sadie nods and moves to wrap her arms around my neck, burying her face against my throat. "I'm so sorry, Garret. I never wanted to hurt you. I know I have no right to ask, but would you help me do something?" She pulls back and her eyes find mine, the vulnerability on her face killing me.

"Anything."

"Will you come with me so I can file for divorce?"

"Yes. But we're also going to file a restraining order, okay? He's never gonna touch you again, Sadie. I fucking promise. He'll have to go through me, and he won't come out alive."

And I mean every word. Over my dead body will that bastard hurt her again.

CHAPTER SEVENTEEN

SADIE

TELLING GARRET ABOUT GRAHAM WAS HARDER than I imagined. This has not only been the longest day in history, but the most emotionally draining since I lost Mom. I hate knowing there's still so much I need to tell him, but for now, things seem okay. Garret's been close by me all day, and I love that about him, but I need just a few minutes of alone time.

We came back to his place about an hour ago, and while he takes a shower, I'm relaxing on his back porch swing. The cool breeze swirls around me, and I bask in the silence of his property.

My cell phone beeps from the spot next to me, a text from my mom's lawyer. I called him after dropping the box off at Garret's, but he didn't answer, so I left him a lengthy and tear-filled voicemail.

Mitchell: I'm proud of you, Sadie. I'll get the papers drawn up and sent to you Monday.

Sadie: Thank you. Garret is going to help me file a restraining order.

Mitchell: Good.

Sadie: I'll talk to you on Monday, okay?

Mitchell: Sounds good.

Locking the screen, I place it back down and pump my legs, my bare feet nowhere near the deck. Leaning my head back against the cushion, I close my eyes and just enjoy the moment. For the first time in what feels like forever, I can finally breathe.

Everything is going to be okay.

The sound of the slider door has my eyes opening. Garret steps onto the porch in a pair of cotton shorts and an old Walker's Taphouse tee. He has a piece of paper in his hand as he comes over to me. "I was gonna order dinner. You feel like pizza?"

"Sure. Where are you getting it from?"

"That place over on Memorial. They have the best Hawaiian in town."

"Okay."

"Be right back."

He goes inside to place the order and when he comes back out, I move my phone so there's room for him. Garret sits and puts a leg behind me, pulling me back against his chest.

"Should be here in twenty minutes."

"Perfect."

"Sadie." Every time he says my name, I get a tingly feeling, something I never felt when he was calling me Nacole. Now he knows who I am, and there's no more pretending.

"What?"

"There's something I need to say, so just listen for a minute, all right?" I nod and he kisses the back of my neck. "I know my anger this morning scared you, and I can't stop feeling like the world's biggest dick."

I turn to face him and he kisses my nose. "I wasn't—"

"I saw the look on your face, and while it didn't register until after, I know what I saw. You know I would never hurt you, right? You're safe with me."

"I know that, Garret. You're a good man."

"I'm so sorry for scaring you. Forgive me."

I trace a finger along his jaw, then give him a soft kiss. "Nothing to forgive. I deserved the anger, and I know you wouldn't hurt me like that. I trust you with everything I have."

"I'd die before laying a finger on you in anger."

"I know."

Dinner arrives soon after, and we eat on the porch, the night air calm and quiet.

Hours later, I lie awake in bed next to him, his soft snores filling the room. Even in the dark room, I can make out his features, and I just stare at him, completely content. He's on his back in just a pair of boxer briefs, the blanket pulled down to his waist. Rolling toward him, I sling my arm over him, and in his sleep, he pulls me closer. Closing my eyes, I try to sleep but I just can't. Restless, I shift around until I'm more comfortable, and I hear Garret's husky chuckle.

"If you wanted to get laid, you could've just asked, baby," he mumbles, and his arm comes down to rub up and down my bare thigh.

My skin prickles with goose bumps and I laugh. "You wish, buddy."

Rolling over, I try to get comfortable once more, but Garret scoots behind me, grabbing my hip to pull me back against him. His erection presses against my lower back and I groan, shifting my hips back on it. He laughs and pulls me back even farther, slipping his arm under my head, cradling me to him.

"I think you wish too, babe."

His hand on my hip slowly slides up my side, only stopping when he reaches the shirt I wore to bed, slipping under it. The second his hand makes contact with my bare breast, I'm done for. His fingertips tease the side of my breast, my breath coming in shallow pants. His hips flex with his movement, and I rock back against him, the sound of his quiet groans causing my heart to race.

"Garret…."

"Yeah, baby?"

"I need you."

"Yeah?"

"Inside. Right now. Please."

Turning my face to him, he takes my mouth with a passion that causes my stomach to clench. I'm soaking wet and trembling with the need for him to fill me.

"Take off your panties. Now."

His weight against my back is gone, and I do as he says. The sound of the end table opening has me spreading my legs, the ache unbearable. Not wanting to wait, I trail my hand down my body and don't stop until I'm running my middle finger through my wetness, circling my clit. Biting down on my bottom lip, I let out a moan and Garret growls from the side of the bed.

"You better not be doing what I think you're doing."

"Hurry up," I moan, my fingers moving harder and faster, my hips bucking on their own accord. Garret is on the bed in seconds, rolling me back over to my side. Moving behind me, he grabs my leg and pulls it over his hip, opening me to him. His calloused hand comes around my waist and dips down, teasing my body. One of his fingers runs down to where I need him most and traces around my clit, barely applying any pressure.

"Garret…."

That same finger moves down to my opening and he slides it inside, hooking his finger on every pump. Throwing my head back, I gasp when he adds a second finger, pumping in time to the thrusting of my hips. His thumb attacks my clit at the same time, and I bite down on the back of my hand. Just before I go falling over the edge, he removes his hand and I feel him fumbling around behind me. The thick head of his cock nudges me from behind and I arch my back, making it easier for him to slip in.

"Shit," he groans, and now it's my turn to laugh.

"You okay back there?"

"So fucking good," he tells me, hips beginning a lazy thrust. Keeping me cradled in his arms, he takes me with long, slow strokes, setting my body on fire with each one. It's obvious from the sounds we're both making that this won't last long. We're too worked up.

"Harder," I demand, but he shakes his head, pressing his cheek to my shoulder.

"No, I want this to last. It'll be over in a heartbeat if I go any faster."

"Please," I whine, and he moves impossibly slower.

"You're so fucking beautiful," he rasps, lips sliding to the back of my neck. He releases my hip to flick my clit in time with his thrusts, and I cry out, my body tightening. I know it won't be much longer.

"That's it, baby. You're so close."

I have no idea how he knows my body so well, but I don't question it. His thumb begins making hard, fast circles and I'm coming, his name vibrating off the walls with my release. His wet lips press between my shoulder blades, and the harsh breaths against my skin tell me he's just as close.

Taking my only free hand, I reach behind me and run my fingers over the sensitive skin of his sac. The moan he releases has my body jerking with an aftershock, and I run my fingernails over the tight skin.

"Fuck." With a handful of hard thrusts, his hand tightens on my waist and he jerks me back against him, bottoming out with a harsh groan, his release tearing through his body. Garret's hips jerk against me as he rides out his orgasm, and I go limp, my entire body wrung out.

Lying together, we both pant and I start giggling.

"Care to tell me why you're laughing when your boyfriend is still inside of you?"

"I have no idea," I tell him.

He pulls out, dropping a kiss to my lips. "Goofball."

Climbing off the bed, he moves to the bathroom and I roll over, grabbing my discarded panties from the floor. Pulling them on, I yank the blankets over me, my eyes now heavy and tired.

I'm falling into a deep sleep when Garret's deep voice washes over me.

"Night, sweetheart."

§

A week later, I head into work and go straight for Brody's office. Knocking on the door, I'm told to come in, so I open it and step inside.

"Hey, Brody, I was wondering if you had a minute to talk?" I ask.

Brody motions to the chair across from him and I sit down. Almost three months ago, I was sitting here interviewing for a job, and now I sit here ready to tell him the truth.

"What's on your mind, Nacole?"

Taking a deep breath, I reach into my purse and pull

out my license, placing it on the desk in front of him. He gives me a look of confusion.

"My full name is Sadie Nacole Ward. I moved here from San Diego to get away from my abusive husband of seven years. I'm filing for divorce tomorrow, and I'm falling in love with your brother. I've been lying since the day I walked in here, and if you want to fire me, I completely understand. But I told Garret the truth, and it's time I told you too. I'm sorry, Brody, and I hope you can find it in your heart to forgive me."

The words spill out of my mouth in a rush, and I look up to see Brody staring at me, an unrecognizable look on his face. Then his features morph into sadness.

"Well fuck."

I look down at my hands, knowing I have to face the consequences.

"Are you okay?"

His words shock me, and I look back up at him.

"What?"

"I can't imagine how scared you must've been, moving here to start over, all alone. And I know you said before that you lost your mom suddenly beforehand too."

"Yeah. It was terrifying, but I had to get away from him."

"I'm glad you did. I know it must be hard to come clean, but you have a ton of people in your corner. We're all behind you, 100 percent."

"Thank you. I'm so glad I met you all. It's been life changing."

"Yeah, I get the feeling you've been pretty life changing for that brother of mine," he says with a laugh, and I blush, my cheeks on fire.

"I hope so."

"Trust me. I have never seen my brother the way he is with you. For so long, his career was his life. And don't get me wrong, if he makes detective, it'll only cement that, but I think you're it for him. I see it in his face when he talks about you."

"We'll see," I tell him, standing.

Brody gets up so he can come hug me, then holds me out at arm's length. "I'm glad you told me. Don't ever be afraid to confide in me or Linds. We got you."

I turn to leave when he grabs my arm.

"Oh, and Sadie? It's nice to finally meet the real you." He winks and sits back down at his desk.

Leaving his office, I head out to the bar area to grab an apron. Tying it around my waist, I turn when the bell jingles on the door. Nate, the night manager and bartender, comes walking in, a backpack over his shoulder. I wave to him and head over to my first table of the night.

"Hi, I'm Sadie, and I'll be taking care of you this evening. Can I start you off with something to drink?"

And with that one sentence, I find myself again.

§

"Hey, you." Garret steps inside my living room, a

black duffel in his hand. Jumping off the couch, I launch myself at him and he grabs me, my legs winding around his waist. He gives me a quick kiss and laughs when I smile against his mouth. "Miss me?"

"Mmhmm. I made dinner. Are you hungry?"

"Starving. What'd you make?"

"Chicken parmesan."

"Sounds perfect." Tossing his bag on the couch, he walks behind me into the kitchen. I set the table, the food still hot since I just took it out of the oven. Grabbing the plates, I hand him one and he digs in. I reach into the fridge for a couple of water and set them down, moving to grab my own food when he pulls me onto his lap, cupping my cheek.

"Thank you for dinner, babe. I appreciate it so much."

"Of course."

I wrap my arm around his shoulders and press my forehead to his. Garret is always going out of his way to thank me for the little things, making sure I know how much he appreciates me. How much he cares about me. It's something I haven't felt in a very long time, and it's certainly making me fall harder for him every day. I'd be lying if I said I wasn't in love with him, because I have no doubt in my mind. How could I not?

He's the most incredible person I've ever known, and each day with him is like a tiny slice of my own heaven. I know he's in love with me too, but we've never actually spoken those words. But he doesn't need to. He says them every day in the way he acts. The way he holds doors open for me, makes me breakfast on the weekend, and always holds me every night.

And I know my mom would've loved him.

Rising from his lap, I grab myself some dinner and bring it back to the table, sitting across from him. I take a bite and groan, chicken parm one of my favorite meals.

"Are you working tomorrow night?" Garret asks, taking a sip of water.

"Nope. Why?"

"Hunter is having a huge get-together, and Brody was passing on a message from him that we're invited. I know you and Carmen get along well."

"I'd love to go," I say, cutting another bite of chicken.

"Great." Garret's grin is infectious, and I smile back at him.

"What?"

"Nothing. You've just… I don't know. You're so different lately."

"Different?"

"That was a bad choice of words. You just seem so—"

"Happy?"

Garret nods and leans back in his chair. "Yeah. Like this huge weight was lifted off your shoulders. And I gotta say, I love everything about it."

"It's because of you, you nut. You're what makes me so happy."

"Same here, Sades."

Sades. Well that's new. And I love it.

§

"Graham, stop. Please, I'm sorry, I didn't mean to."

He knocks me to the ground, his foot connecting with a painful kick to my side. Crying, I roll over and clutch myself, curling into the fetal position.

"You fuck everything up, Sadie. Goddamn useless piece of shit. I ask you to do one thing and you can't even manage to not screw it up. Christ, I don't know how to get through to you."

I force myself up, pain searing through my side, and I cry out. "It wasn't my fault. I told you the truth. They said your suit was mixed up with another order, and by the time I called it was too late. You have other suits, Graham."

"Shut the fuck up," he shouts, enunciating each word with a slap to my face, skin reddened with the hits. Turning on his heel, he leaves me alone in the bedroom, crying and broken.

Crawling to the end table, I find my cell phone and start to dial my mom, but then I remember. She's gone. Never coming back.

And I'm all alone with Graham.

Jolting awake, I sit up straight, clutching my chest and breathing heavy from the terror of my dream. Swinging my legs over the side of the bed, I try to get myself under control, counting to ten, taking deep breaths. Folding over, I bury my face in my hands and will the tears to go away. It feels like all I've done lately is cry, and I'm so sick of it.

I'm just getting myself together when a warm hand touches my back, causing me to jump in fright.

"Shit, I'm sorry. Are you okay?"

Sniffling, I climb back into bed and roll over, my face tucked into Garret's chest.

"Yeah, bad dream is all. I didn't mean to wake you up."

"Nothing to be sorry for."

Garret runs his fingers through my hair and we lie together in silence, my brain running a thousand miles a minute. I'm tired, but I can't fall asleep.

"You wanna talk about it?" he mumbles, and I shake my head.

"No."

"Babe, can I ask you something?"

"Sure."

Garret moves to rest on an elbow and peers down at me. "Have you thought about talking to somebody? A professional?"

"I already do. Carmen recommended her, and I've been seeing her once a week."

"How's it going?"

"Well, I'm here, aren't it?" I joke, and Garret pulls me back to his chest.

"Yeah, thank fuck for that."

"Can I ask you something?" I whisper.

"Anything."

"Dr. Klein asked if you would sit in on one of our sessions sometime. I'm always able to talk about everything best when she's with me. Makes me feel extra safe. Would you come?"

"Of course, if that's what you want."

I burrow into his chest and listen to the thumping of his heart. "Dr. Klein thinks I need to share the things I've been keeping inside, and that I can't really move past everything until I do. So yeah, it's what I want."

"Then I'm there, baby."

He kisses my head, and we drift off to sleep in each other's arms. My dreams are peaceful, no part of my past chasing me for the rest of the night.

§

Switching off the light, I step from the bathroom into Garret's bedroom and head for where I left my sandals. Slipping them on my feet, I look up to see him watching me from the doorway.

"What?" I ask, tucking my hair behind my ear.

"You look stunning, Sades."

I glance down at my outfit: jean shorts and a hunter-green tank top. Entirely basic.

"Thanks." I blush.

Coming into the bedroom, he kisses my cheek and goes into the bathroom. He comes out a minute later, putting his watch on, and the scent of his cologne washes over me.

"Ready to roll?"

I nod and reach for the sweatshirt I left lying on his

bed, folding it over my arm. We head downstairs and out to his truck, Garret locking the door behind him. I offered to drive tonight so he could drink with his buddies, so he holds the driver door open for me and we take off, the latest Keith Urban single blasting through the stereo.

Since I've been to Hunter and Carmen's before, the drive is easy and in no time, we're turning into the driveway, a bunch of other vehicles out front. Parking next to a large Ford, I shut the engine off and fiddle with my keys in my lap.

"Everything okay?" Garret asks, turning toward me, reaching out to calm my hands.

"I'm just realizing this is the first time I'll see your friends since that barbeque Brody had. They met Nacole, not Sadie. What am I supposed to say to them?"

Understanding dawns on Garret's face, and his thumb runs circles on the back of my hand. "Yeah, I had a feeling you'd be worried about that. I called Brody this morning, asked him to make sure everyone knew, but not to get into it with them. It's nobody's business unless you want them to know the details, okay?"

"Thank you, Garret."

"Hey, you're my girl. It's my job to take care of you."

Kissing his cheek, I climb out of the car and grab my sweatshirt from the back seat. Taking my hand in his, Garret walks us to the front door, ringing the doorbell when we reach it.

Carmen swings the door open a moment later with a huge smile followed by the tightest hug I've ever received.

"I'm so glad you came, girl. Garret, thank you for coming too." She reaches up to hug Garret and he pats her back, still holding tightly to my hand.

Yeah, that boyfriend of mine is one protective man. And I wouldn't change a thing about him. I've never felt so loved or wanted in my entire life.

Carmen ushers us inside and brings us out to the backyard where a large crowd of people are hanging out. I notice Brody and Lindsey, and the other couple I met, Kennedy and Grayson, but there are others here I don't know.

Garret squeezes my hand and looks down to wink at me. Bringing us over to Brody, he hugs his brother and Lindsey embraces me, whispering in my ear how proud she and Brody are of me. My cheeks heat at her words, and then Carmen drags us over to the people I don't know.

She gestures to a really tall guy with blue eyes and a backward baseball cap, and he gives her a side hug. "Sadie, this is my older brother, Noah, and his wife, Aubrey. Guys, this is Garret's girl, Sadie."

"Hey, so nice to finally meet you." Noah shakes my hand and Aubrey does the same, the petite blonde absolutely stunning. Carmen then grabs the other two men standing nearby. "And this is Aubrey's brother, Landon, and his husband, Chase. Noah and Chase are firefighters at the same station as Hunt and Gray."

Landon waves and smiles at me, but Chase steps forward and gives me a bear hug. Laughing, I brush my hair off my face, giving a small wave back at Landon.

"It's nice to meet you all."

Garret shakes hands with the guys, obviously knowing them all, and then he's right back by my side. Brody comes over to the group and smacks Garret on the shoulder, offering him a beer. Garret takes it, and I notice he's still holding my hand.

Is it normal to swoon over your own boyfriend?

Carmen hands me a bottled water and then drags me away from Garret to the other women, creating our own group. I give Garret a sympathetic glace and he feigns being sad. I roll my eyes and turn back to the girls.

"Okay, so you have to give us the scoop." Kennedy says, taking a sip of her red wine.

"Scoop on what?" I ask, twisting the cap on my water.

"Girl, Aubrey and I have known this crew the longest—most of them, anyway—and Garret has always been the dark horse. No girlfriend, nothing. And your ass hooked him. Hard core. He can't stop looking over here to see you. So, we need all the details."

"I don't know. There's not much to tell, really. He's just amazing. I know that seems vague, but it's true. He's incredible. He's my own personal hero. And he hasn't done anything but make me fall in love with him."

A loud shout from behind me has us all turning, only to find Grayson horsing around with Garret. Gray has about three inches on Garret, so he easily pulls him to the ground, all the other guys hooting and hollering.

"Oh, for crying out loud, Gray. Grow up," Kennedy

groans, and we all laugh.

"What's going on?" Carmen asks Hunter, and he flexes his muscles at her.

"Mr. Tough Cop here thinks Gray isn't getting in a good enough pump at the station gym, so he bet him that he couldn't bench press him."

"What the hell is wrong with you guys?" Carmen laughs, shaking her head. Gray gets off the ground and tries to lift Garret, but instead he gets a knee to the balls, dropping with a loud shout.

"Oh please, I barely knocked those babies. They're so far up there's no way I hurt you that bad." Garret jokes, laughing when Gray kicks at him.

Garret pulls himself off the ground, brushing his shirt off, but Brody grabs him around the neck, rubbing his fist on his head.

"Brody, what the hell, man?"

"Not so tough, are you, bro?"

"Not when you're trying to rub a hole in my skull, fucker. Get off."

But Brody doesn't let up, and in seconds Garret fights against him, yelling loudly.

"Pineapple! Pineapple, asshole!"

Brody releases him and gives him a strange look. "What?"

"Pineapple is my safe word. Now back off."

Covering my mouth with my hand, I start cracking up, Carmen dying next to me as well. Everyone is soon laughing along with us, and Garret just looks at everyone with a questioning glare.

"What's so funny?" he asks, looking over at Brody, who seems just as lost.

"Dude, you just safe-worded your little brother. Didn't know you guys rolled that way." Hunter lets out a loud whoop and Garret starts laughing, realizing his mistake.

"Fuck no, that's nasty," he replies, and Hunter just shrugs.

"It's cool, man. Carmen's safe word is—"

"Hunter!"

Carmen is standing there with her hands on her hips, a murderous look in her eyes. Hunter pretends to lock his lips and she nods, laughing when Noah pretends to kill himself.

"I have an idea," I say, and everyone turns to look at me. "Siblings on opposite sides of the room. None of you can be trusted."

Brody laughs loudly and smacks Garret on the back. "I told you I liked this one, bro."

Garret strides over to me and gives me a fast kiss, his smile wide and infectious.

The rest of the evening is filled with laughter and antics from the guys. I spend it with the girls, talking about anything and everything. I finally give in and tell them a bit about me and Garret, and by the end of the evening, I know I've found my place.

CHAPTER EIGHTEEN

GARRET

Stepping into the precinct, I find Jace at my desk, pacing in circles. He looks up and when he notices me, a huge smile breaks out on his face.

"Dude, where have you been?"

I check my watch and raise my eyebrows. "Well, I was due on shift at 9:00 a.m. and it's 9:02 a.m., so I'm walking inside?"

"Chief left a letter on your desk about ten minutes ago."

"Okay?"

"*Dude*. A *letter*?" Jace is staring at me like I have seven heads.

I toss my bag onto my chair, reaching for the envelope sitting on my desk. I still have no idea what his issue is, so I rip the letter open and hold it up. It takes me thirty seconds to read it, but I have to keep rereading it until it sinks in.

"So? What is it, man?"

"I passed."

Jace gives me all of .2 seconds before he's cheering loudly, pulling me into a hug huge. "Fuck yes!" he shouts, climbing onto my desk. "Excuse me, can I have everyone's attention, please?"

The other officers in the room all look his way, laughing at his crazy antics.

"My partner and best friend of ten years passed the detective's exam!"

Everyone starts clapping and I shake my head at him, currently doing the floss on top of my desk.

Dropping into my chair, I lean back and keep reading the words in the letter. I'm floored. Not that I didn't think I had what it takes, but still. I fucking did it.

Jace hops down and sits on top, looking at me with a smile. "I'm proud of you, Garret. You've worked your ass off, and I couldn't be happier for you. You know we gotta celebrate, right?"

"Yeah, we will. Definitely. You mind covering for me for a second?"

"Yeah, man. Go call your girl. I got your back."

Slapping his arm, I duck out and walk down to the hallway near the bathrooms where it's quiet. Taking my phone from my back pocket, I pull up Sadie's number and hit FaceTime. It only rings for a few seconds and she answers, bare-faced and fucking beautiful.

"Garret?"

"Hey, babe. You got a sec?"

"For you? Always. What's up?"

Leaning my back against the wall, I try to find the right words but I can't, so I just blurt them out. "So when I came in, Jace was pacing like a caged animal waiting for me."

Her eyebrows rise. "Everything okay?"

"Yeah. I fucking passed, Sades. I did it."

Her brown eyes widen in shock, and she covers her mouth with her hand. "I knew you would. I'm so damn proud of you."

Jace said those words to me only a few minutes ago, but coming from her mouth, they make me feel even better. Making my girl proud is top of my priority list, always.

"Thanks, baby."

Her eyes are teary and she laughs at herself. "I'm such a mess, and it's not even my news. Hope you're up for a serious celebration tonight."

"Yeah, you better be in bed when I get back this afternoon."

"Oh yes, with bells and whistles."

"Sadie Ward has a kinky side. Who knew?" I joke, and she bursts out laughing.

"Yeah, I'm real dangerous. Listen, I was about to jump in the shower, but call me later if you get a chance, okay?"

"You know it. Have a good day, Sades."

She blows me a kiss, and then the call ends. It was on the tip of my tongue to tell her how much I love her, but I haven't. I may be celebrating passing the exam, but I'm not saying "I love you" for the first time over a video chat.

No, that's not happening.

§

Finishing the last of my paperwork, I stretch back in my chair and look up to see Jace walking over in street clothes.

"You almost done?"

"Yeah, in another ten minutes or so. Why?"

"Just wondering. You sure I can't tempt you into going out for a drink?"

I shake my head and toss my pen down. "Tomorrow night. I really just wanna get home to Sadie."

Jace chuckles and scrubs a hand down his face. "Can't argue with that. Congrats again, buddy. Say hi to your girl for me."

Bumping my fist with his, he takes off and I get back to work.

Twenty minutes later, I'm heading home. After hitting the buttons on my dash, the sound of ringing fills my Jeep, and a second later Sadie answers.

"Hey, Garret."

"Hey, baby. I'm about ten minutes from my place. What time are you coming over tonight?"

"Shit. Hold on a second."

A loud commotion in the background has me narrowing my eyes, and then she's back on the line. "Hey, listen, I'm so sorry but Caroline called out and Brody needed me. I'm working till ten."

"Oh."

"I'm sorry, Garret. I know you wanted to celebrate tonight, but I didn't want to say no to your brother. Please don't be angry with me."

"No, I'm not angry, babe. I understand. I'm disappointed, but it's fine. Jace was gonna take me out to get a drink, but I turned him down. Maybe I'll just go anyway."

"Well, why don't you come here? I want to buy you a drink, okay?"

I can't let her down, so I agree and end the call, figuring I can get changed and go. It's only just after five, so the bar shouldn't be too packed, and then I can head out with Jace.

Pulling into my driveway, I switch off the engine and send a quick text to Jace. He agrees to meet me at Walker's, and I head inside to shower and change.

Fifteen minutes later, I stroll out of my house. The drive to my brother's bar doesn't take too long, and soon enough I'm parking in the lot.

Locking my Jeep, I head inside, spinning my baseball hat backward. I pull the door open and am immediately overcome by the loud cheers and shouts.

"*Congratulations!*"

Well I'll be damned.

Standing in front of me is everybody I love. My parents and Brody are next to the bar, and all my coworkers are there, Jace included. And off to the side is the most beautiful woman I've ever met in my life. And fuck, does she look good. She's clapping softly, and I don't miss the sparkle in her eyes.

Brody comes over to me first and gives me a hard hug, cupping the back of my head.

"So fucking proud of you, bro."

"Thanks, Brody. What is all this?"

"Sadie called me this morning, and we got it all thrown together."

I shake my head at him in disbelief, and then my mom comes swooping over to me, throwing her arms around my neck. "Hey, Momma."

"We couldn't be prouder of you, sweetheart. Congratulations."

"Love y'all."

When I shake my dad's hand, he looks off to the side and finds me still staring at my girl. "Go see that pretty thing of yours. She's one hell of a lady."

"Thanks, Dad."

Leaving my parents behind, I make my way toward Sadie. When I get a foot away, she rushes me and jumps into my arms. I catch her easily, hoisting her up so her legs go around my waist. Burying my face in her neck, I breathe her in and close my eyes.

"Thank you," I say quietly, and she pulls away, kissing me hard in front of everybody, earning a few whistles.

"Of course. And for the record, I've had this planned since you told me about the test."

"How is that possible?"

"I told Brody that when you found out, we were

throwing you a surprise party, and he was hosting it, and he better like it."

"Sassy. I like this side of you. But how'd you know I'd pass?"

"Oh please, Garret. I know you better than you think. I knew you would because you're the best person I know and you're incredibly smart. You can do anything if you put your mind to it."

Holding her tight with one arm, I cup her cheek with my other hand, forehead pressed to hers. "What the hell did I do to deserve someone like you?"

"I ask myself the same thing every day."

Looking deep into her eyes, I lick my lips and then kiss her again. She tastes like home.

"I love you, Sadie."

She doesn't look shocked, and even though I see the tears shining in her eyes, I know they aren't sad ones.

"I love you too, Garret. So much."

Placing her down on her feet, it's only then I notice something different about her.

"Hey, when'd you do this?" I ask, fingering her now much shorter hair. It's just above her shoulders, and while it's different, it also looks good. More elegant, somehow.

"I like it," I say, and she laughs.

"I did it to celebrate."

"You cut your hair because I passed the detective's exam?"

She shakes her head. "No, I did it because Graham was served the restraining order, and Mitchell said the divorce should be final in ninety days. He pulled some strings once he filed all the evidence of abuse."

"Fuck yeah," I growl, pulling her mouth to mine, completely devouring her in front of all our friends and family. Her tongue pushes into my mouth and I groan, her hands banding around my waist.

When I pull away, she looks up at me, flushed and breathless.

"Get a room!" Brody yells, and everybody starts laughing, us included.

Taking her hand, I bring her with me over to the bar and order a round of drinks for everybody. Sadie grabs a bottled water and winks at me, then blows me a kiss.

Together, we all celebrate. Surrounded by the most important people in my life, my girl by my side, I know life couldn't get any better.

Or so I think.

§

Hours later, I step in the front door of my house, Sadie tangled in my arms. She followed me over here, and now I need to get her in my bed.

Kicking the door shut behind us, I pick her up and her legs tighten around my waist, my hands clutching her ass. Stumbling up the stairs, I make it to my bedroom and toss her on the bed, her laughter filling the room. Toeing off my boots, I rip my shirt over my head and drag my pants down, falling onto the bed on top of her.

My mouth attacks hers in an aggressive kiss, her breathing coming in quick pants. Nipping her bottom lip, I pull it between my teeth, causing a moan to break from her throat, her hips thrusting against mine. Leaning up on my knees, I yank her pants down while she pulls her shirt off. Beginning at the swell between her breasts, I work my way down, tongue swirling around her belly button.

Sadie sits up and with her hand grips the hair on the back of my head. I slip her underwear off and spread her legs, running my tongue along the inside of her thigh. I spread her for me and my mouth waters, needing my taste now.

"Garret—"

She breaks off when I lick straight up to her clit, sucking it roughly into my mouth. I'm not gentle as I devour her, my tongue and fingers moving in sync with each other. Curling my fingers, I stroke the spot that makes her shatter every single time. I'm greedy for her pleasure, and I need her to come now.

I can tell the second she does, her body taut and her back arching. My name ricochets off the walls, and her grip on my hair tightens to the point of painful.

Wiping my mouth on the inside of her thigh, I straighten up, my cock aching to be inside of her. Reaching over to the end table, I grab a condom and rip it open, rolling it down my shaft as fast as I can.

"How do you want me?" she teases, sitting up to unhook her bra.

"You're trying to fucking kill me, woman."

"Nah, I'm just really turned on, and I have this hot-as-hell man in front of me."

"Oh, well say no more, then."

Climbing onto the bed, I slide her down so she's in the center, then flip her onto her stomach. Moving behind her, I take advantage and run my hands down her spine to that perfect ass. Gripping the base of my cock, I rub the head up and down her wetness, teasing her clit on every slide.

"Stop screwing around back there," she groans and I take mercy on her, driving in balls deep on the first thrust, causing us both to moan in unison. I start a steady pace, reaching up to grip her shoulder, the other hand on her hip. The bed shakes with the force of my thrusts, and she cries out with each.

"Fuckin hell," I moan, head dropping back onto my shoulders. Her pussy is gripping me so tight, and I know she's close to coming again, so I slow my thrusts, not wanting this to end yet. I slip my arms under her body and pull her upright so her back is flush with my chest.

Sadie's head falls back onto my shoulder and I bite down on her bare shoulder, my free hand cupping her breast, fingers pinching her hardened nipple.

"Oh my God, Garret. Yes."

"So good, baby."

Grunting louder than before, I begin canting my hips harder, the hand on her breast slipping down to finger her clit. The tingling in my spine is growing stronger, and I can't hold on for much longer. Moving both hands to her thighs, I spread her legs even wider and slam into her as hard as I can, her cries turning into shouts as she begins to milk my cock, coming harder than she did before.

The harsh groan I release vibrates off her skin, and I bury my face in the crook of her neck, my release tearing through me, my legs shaking with the pleasure. Slowly I lower her onto the bed and pull out, falling next to her.

Panting, she turns in my arms and kisses my bare chest.

"Fuck, that was good," I tell her, running a hand up and down her sweaty back.

She laughs and rests her head on my chest, tangling her legs with mine. A moment later, I force myself to climb off the bed and take care of the condom, returning with a warm washcloth so I can clean her up. After throwing it into the hamper, I come back into the bedroom to find her lying in the middle of the bed wearing the T-shirt I had on tonight.

"Aw, did I wear someone out?"

"Yes, you and that giant dick," she whines, rolling over when I climb in behind her.

"Well, my giant dick and I are more than happy to oblige."

"So lucky I love you, jackass," she mutters.

Within minutes I hear her breathing even out, and I know she's asleep.

"Yeah, baby. I really am." Placing a kiss to the top of her head, I pull her close and settle down, falling asleep almost instantly, dreaming of the short-haired beauty in my arms.

CHAPTER NINETEEN

SADIE

It's been three weeks since Garret passed his detective's exam, and life couldn't be better. He's coming to my therapy appointment tonight finally, and I'm starting to get nervous about it. I know what Dr. Klein wants me to come clean about, because I've only given her slight hints about the one thing I can't get past. To be honest, I don't think I ever will. And I'm scared to see Garret's reaction.

Pulling my short hair back into a ponytail as best as I can manage, I head back into my living room, reaching for my purse on the couch. Today is also my day off from work, so I'm off to run errands. I want to make something different for dinner tonight, and I'm armed with my mom's recipe book, hoping there's something in there Garret will love. He's very much a meat-and-potatoes kind of guy, but my mom made amazing food.

Driving to the local grocery store, I notice a car

following me. They've been behind me almost since I left my house. Knowing it's just my imagination, I focus on the road and breathe a sigh of relief when I turn into the parking lot and the car continues on.

It's clear I'm on edge with the anxiety of tonight, and I wish Garret wasn't at work. Just being with him calms my entire being, and right now I need that. But since I can't have it, I'll settle for baking the day away.

Parking near the entrance, I hurry inside, my decision made about both dinner and dessert: mom's recipe for baked mac and cheese and a simple blueberry pie. It's closing in on early fall, so it'll be perfect.

Grabbing a shopping cart, I begin loading it up with what I need when my phone dings with a text from Garret.

Garret: Tonight will be fine, sweetheart.

Sadie: How'd you know?

Garret: Just a feeling I had. I told you, I'm in this. Nothing you say will ruin that.

Sadie: I love you.

Garret: Feeling's pretty mutual. I'll meet you there tonight.

Sadie: See you then.

Guiding the cart through the store, it doesn't take me long to get everything I need. Ten minutes later, I'm leaving the store with a handful of bags, the sun shining brightly. Popping the trunk, I get everything inside and slam it shut.

Heading back home, I pull into my driveway and park the car, carrying everything inside. Placing all the bags on the counter, I plug my cell phone into the wireless speaker and crank some Blake Shelton. Dancing around, I begin work on the pie, putting everything I need for dinner in the fridge and cabinets.

An hour later, the house smells like heaven and it's almost two in the afternoon. Our appointment with Dr. Klein is at four thirty, so I decide to get ready now.

Hurrying through a shower and blow-drying my hair, I forego any makeup and dress in a pair of legging and an oversized sweater. Swinging into my bedroom to grab the latest paperback I've been reading, I get comfortable on my couch, flip to where I last read, and settle in.

§

Pulling into the parking lot of Dr. Klein's office, I spot Garret's Jeep toward the back, his frame leaning against the side of it. Parking next to him, I climb out and he puts his cell back into his pocket, smiling at me.

"Hey, beautiful."

"Hi. You ready?"

"Yeah. Are you?" He reaches out to play with a strand of my hair, and I can't help myself. Stepping forward, I wrap my arms around his waist, taking a deep breath, his cologne the only thing I can smell.

"Yeah, I am," I say into his chest, rising on tiptoes to kiss him.

He takes my hand and we stroll inside. While my nerves are high and I'm silently freaking out, I know this is the best thing for me. For us. Every week, I spend an hour talking to Dr. Klein about some of the hardest moments of my marriage, and while she knows each and every one, we still talk about it in depth, finding a way for me to move on has been hard.

Arriving in the lobby, we make our way to the receptionist and I give her my name. The woman tells us Dr. Klein will be with us shortly.

Garret walks us over to a group of chairs and we sit. My knee bounces up and down, and he snakes an arm around my shoulders, pulling me in close.

When she comes out to greet us a few minutes later, Garret squeezes me and we head into the room.

Dr. Klein smiles warmly. "Garret, thank you for joining us today. It's so nice to meet you."

"Thanks, ma'am. It's nice to meet you as well."

Garret sits next to me on the couch and Dr. Klein takes a seat across from us, a notebook on her lap. "So, Sadie and I have been seeing each other now for a couple months, and after we discussed the basis of why she came here, every week we talk about something that's been painful for her to move on from. Her mother is a large topic that we discuss every time."

My eyes are already burning. Garret leans his elbows

on his knees, reaching out for my hand. "Yeah, when she told me about her passing, we spent a few days together talking."

"She told me that. Now, Sadie, is there anything you would like to talk about?"

"I do, but I'm just unsure of what to begin with," I respond.

"You can tell me anything, babe. I told you that," Garret says.

I nod at him and release his hand, moving over on the couch so we're no longer touching.

"Sorry, I need space for this."

"It's okay."

"So, Garret, from what I gather, you and your family have a good relationship?" Dr. Klein asks, folding her hands on her lap.

Garret nods. "We do. I have a younger brother and my parents, and we're all very close. Always have been. I grew up in a large family with tons of cousins and aunts and uncles."

"Now, I believe that's Sadie's biggest hardship. She's afraid to take things farther or more seriously, because she doesn't have any family of her own. She doesn't have a way to properly grieve her mother."

Garret looks over his shoulder at me, his eyebrows knit in concern. "What's she talking about, Sades?"

I guess it's now or never.

"I never got to say goodbye to my mom."

"I don't—"

"She was gone when I got to her. Doctors said she had an aneurysm and there was nothing anyone could've done. After the paramedics pronounced her, I went to the hospital where they gave me the items she had on, and they told me they'd be in contact after the autopsy."

Tears are already pouring down my cheeks, and I can tell how badly Garret wants to have me in his arms.

"Okay. So what happened? Why didn't you get to say goodbye?"

"Because Graham took her away from me. He ruined everything." Reaching for a tissue on the coffee table in front of us, I wipe my eyes and try to get control of myself, but I can't.

"I don't understand, sweetheart."

Forcing my eyes to Garret's, I clench my hands together, gently rocking back and forth.

"I lost my mom. I was inconsolable and wasn't able to deal with anything. I didn't take calls, because I needed just a little bit of time. Just a few days. I wanted to have a service for her, to have a burial so I could have a place for her. To visit her, to miss her."

"That's understandable. So what happened next, Sadie?" Dr. Klein presses, writing something in her notebook.

"Graham wouldn't pay for it. Said she wasn't his mother, so why should he waste his money?"

"What an asshole," Garret grumbles, and I can't help the tiny laugh I let out.

"I begged and pleaded with him. I told him I hated

him, and he didn't like that. Grabbed me by the throat and threw me against the wall."

Garret's hands clench into fists, but I ignore it and push on. "He told me I had no idea what hate was, and that I could go down to the morgue and get my mom from the—"

My voice breaks and I fold over, crying into my knees. Garret rubs a hand up and down my back and just lets me cry, silent while I work through my emotions.

"It's okay, Sadie. But you need to let this out and find a way through it. It's eating you alive, and you need to let go of the guilt. Embrace the truth that it wasn't your fault."

Dr. Klein's soothing words comfort me, and I sit up straight, knowing she's right.

"I'm okay. Sorry."

"Take your time, baby. We aren't going anywhere." Garret rests his hand on my knee and I grip it tightly, so damn grateful for this man.

"Thank you, Garret."

Grabbing another tissue, I blow my nose and count to ten.

I'm ready. I can do this.

"He told me that while I had been so busy throwing fits, he had taken the call from the funeral home and told them I was unable to speak with them, but that my mother was to be cremated and there would be no service. My mother, the only person who ever really loved me, the only person I could count on, was in a goddamn cardboard box down at the funeral home, and there was nothing I could do. My husband took her away from me, and I never got to tell her how much I loved her. How much I missed her. He took everything from me, and it hurts more than her dying."

Through my tears, I look up to find Garret with his head hanging down, his fingers laced behind it. I can't see his face, but I forge on, needing to say everything.

"That night, after I got home from the funeral home, I put the box in a safe place and went to bed in the guest room. I couldn't even look at him, and to be honest, I didn't trust myself not to murder him. I was so devastated, and I knew no matter what I did, it wouldn't change who he was. I was married to a monster, and I couldn't do anything. I had nobody to live for anymore."

I have to stop to breathe, looking down at the tissues I've shredded. The courage to speak is greater than ever, though I'm still unable to look at Garret, fear of his reaction strong.

"That night, I woke up and found Graham sitting in the armchair next to the bed. He had this menacing smile on his face, and I sat up and told him to get out. I was done with him. Graham came and sat on the bed next to me, and before I could react, he grabbed my arms and pinned me to the bed. He straddled me so I couldn't move and gripped my jaw in one of his hands. He leaned down so he was in my face and told me I was to never speak to him how I had. That I was his wife, and I was to do as he said. I told him I would never forgive him for doing what he'd done."

I finally muster up the courage to look at Garret, and I'm not surprised to find him staring right at me, his eyes red-rimmed and sad.

"He said if I ever did it again, he'd give me something to cry about, and he'd make sure that I wished I was dead like my whore of a mother. I went to bed with bruises on my arms and face, and an even bigger one on my heart. My mom was dead, my husband wished it had been me instead, and I had nowhere to go. Two weeks later, Mitchell Hale called me, letting me know about my mother's life insurance policy and her will. Two months later, I moved here."

Reaching out for Garret's hands, I hold them tightly and look into the blue eyes of my boyfriend. The man I love more than life itself. The man who helped heal me without even knowing it.

"I met you, and I wasn't looking for anything. I convinced myself that I couldn't heal with you. I was scared of you, Garret, and I'm so sorry for that. You're big and tall, and I saw Graham in you so many times. I'm so ashamed of that, because you've been nothing but kind since day one. That's why I reacted that way to you that first night in the bar. I was so scared, and I couldn't help holding you at arm's length. But now I know I was only keeping my future away, and for that I'm so sorry. For over three months, you've done everything you can to make sure I know I have you in my corner, and you were respectful enough to even be friends, no matter how much you wanted more. And I risked all of it because I was scared. I'm so sorry, Garret."

"No."

My eyes widen at his hoarse voice, and he scoots on the couch so he can cup my cheeks, my face only inches from his.

"You don't need to apologize for anything. For a whole month, I talked to you every single day. You told me stories about work. You talked about your favorite things. Every day we talked, and I fell in love with you. I knew there was a chance that you and I would be nothing, but I didn't care. I needed you in my life, Sadie. I needed you. And I still do. I'm not even half the man I want to be without you."

I start to cry, but he doesn't stop. "I'm not sure there are words to ease the pain of what that animal did to your mother. My heart breaks for you, baby, and I wish there was something I could do. But I can promise you this. Every day, I'm going to do everything in my power to show you that you aren't alone. I'm in this with you forever, and I'm never going anywhere. I promise."

His forehead drops to mine and I sob quietly. Finally, I wrap my arms around his neck and allow him to give me the comfort I ache for. He holds me close and doesn't let go, not for even a second.

I've been so scared of disappointing him for so long that I never realized that maybe I hadn't. Maybe I was just what he wanted all along.

Broken pieces and all.

§

Tonight was emotionally exhausting. As I follow Garret on the way to his house, my mind drifts to the session. Despite how hard the whole discussion was, Dr. Klein was right. I feel a sense of peace knowing there are no more secrets about my life, about my past. Garret knows everything, and when he tells me he's in this with me, I believe him.

Turning into his driveway, I park next to him and climb out. My plans for dinner have gone out the window, wanting to just climb under the covers and sleep for ten years.

Garret gets out of his Jeep and meets me in front of my car. He walks me inside, and while he's kicking his boots off, I head up the stairs to his bedroom. Sitting on the edge of the bed, I stare down at the floor, the space between my feet suddenly so interesting.

I see Garret's feet appear a few minutes later, and I look up to his sad eyes staring right at me. He doesn't say anything, just leans against the doorframe, hands shoved in his pockets.

"Do you think Mom was disappointed in me?"

"Of course not. Why would you think that?"

"Well, she wrote me this letter. She left it to me with her will. Said she hated that she never got the chance to get me away from the life I was trapped in, and she was sorry. I tried so hard to hide everything from her because I was so ashamed that I stayed with him. All I could think was that if I hadn't been trying so hard to cover up my bruises with makeup, maybe I'd have gotten to her in time. It's silly, I know."

Garret strides across the room and kneels in front of me, his hands on my thighs.

"Baby, there is no way she was ever disappointed. I think she hurt for you. I certainly do. She was your mother, and no mother wants their child to be abused or treated that way. She loved you, and I have no doubt in my mind that she knew how much you loved her."

I nod and take his hands in mine, throat swelling with emotion. "I did. I loved her so much."

"I know Sades."

"I just miss her so much. I wish she'd met you. I wish she could've seen that I got my happily ever after, you know? It's not fair, Garret."

"Shh, I know. I know. Come here." Garret pulls me down onto his lap and I wind my arms around him, sobbing loudly into his neck. "It wasn't your fault. You need to stop blaming yourself. She wouldn't want that. There was nothing you could've done, and now it's time to move forward. It's time to live, baby."

"I love you," I whisper, clinging to him tighter.

"I love you too. It's gonna be okay, I promise you."

I know it is. Garret doesn't lie.

CHAPTER TWENTY

GARRET

I THINK LIFE IS GETTING BACK TO NORMAL. EVERY day since that session with her therapist three weeks ago, Sadie has made improvement in her grief. I think when the truth came out about her past, she felt tied down by the loss she now had to face head on. Yes, she'd cried to me on her mom's birthday, but I also didn't know the whole story.

It hurt to hear how much pain was involved. Hearing about what that piece of shit did, making a decision about someone he didn't even like, and taking away her only real chance to say goodbye gutted me. I wanted to drive straight to California and beat the holy hell out of him.

Instead, I did what I needed to—I held my girl and promised I'd never let go. And I didn't lie. I meant every fucking word. I need her like I need air, and no matter how corny that sounds, it's the whole and complete truth. We may not have been looking for each other, and she may have fought our attraction, but we were meant to be together. I believe that.

She's so much stronger than she thinks she is. And I'm so damn proud of her.

As I drive down the bumpy dirt road, I glance over at the beauty in the passenger seat. Sadie looks at me with a smile and goes back to singing along with the radio, her short hair stick straight. Reaching over, I tuck it behind her ear and run my thumb down the side of her neck. She takes my hand and rests it in her lap, intertwining our fingers. We're having dinner with my parents tonight, and she's been looking forward to it all day.

I've also been working on a surprise for her, and it should be ready in a couple weeks. It's something she needs, and I hope she loves it.

Turning into my parents' driveway a few minutes later, I park alongside my mom's car and hop down from my Jeep, jogging around the front to open her door. She climbs out and pulls her sweater around her. It's mid-October, and the weather has finally cooled down.

I drape my arm around her shoulder and we make our way inside the house. The door hasn't even shut behind us before I groan out loud. My mom is cooking something that smells amazing, and I'm starving.

"That smells so good," Sadie agrees, and I laugh.

"Hey, we're here!" I announce, finding my parents in the living room watching some movie on television.

Mom jumps up when she hears me and comes rushing over to give us both a huge hug. This woman, I'm telling you. I couldn't ask for a better mother. She has completely welcomed Sadie into the family, and every time we see her, she asks me when she gets to call her another daughter. It makes Sadie cry every time, and I always tell my dad to control his wife.

"You kids hungry? I made roast beef and mashed potatoes."

"God, yes. Fucking starving," I tell her, and she swats my head.

"Language. You may be thirty-three but I can still take you over my knee."

"Ew. You wouldn't dare, Momma."

"Oh wouldn't I?" My mom sticks her hand on her hip and gives me that "mom glare" she's been giving me since I was ten.

I chuckle. "Dad, help your son out here."

Dad laughs from his recliner. "Hell no, son. I don't want to sleep with one eye open tonight."

Momma tsks. "Oh stop it, you fool. Now, if the antics are finished, I have something I'd like to show Sadie, if you don't mind."

Sadie laughs and goes with my mom into the kitchen while I get settled on the couch next to my dad.

He looks over at me and points at the television. "Now I don't have to pretend I understand what'd going on with this movie anymore. Wanna catch the last half of the football game?"

"Do fish swim?" I joke, and Dad changes the channel. Ten minutes later, we're both shouting at the screen, cursing the damn refs for fucking that call up.

Mom and Sadie come back into the room a little bit later holding photo albums, and I know what my mom is doing. She's showing my girlfriend all my embarrassing photos, and Sadie is going to eat it all up.

Thanks a lot, Momma.

§

"No problem. I'll talk to you later, all right?" Jace ends the call and turns back to me. We were sitting in the precinct parking lot, getting ready to head out on shift, when his brother Drew called. I have no idea what's going on.

"What's up?" I ask, taking a sip of coffee.

"Drew and Dad got into another fight."

I shake my head, placing my coffee back in the cupholder. "Again? Now what?"

Drew took over the family business when their dad retired, but it sounds like he's still trying to run the place. They're always at each other's throats.

"I guess Dad showed up when Drew was in the middle of an oil change. When Drew got to his office, the entire place was upended and Dad was trying to reorganize everything, said he can't stand that Drew works in such clutter."

"Sounds like your dad needs to take a long-ass trip to Florida and chill out. Drew's more than capable of running the business."

"Tell that to my dad," Jace groans, then puts the car in

gear, pulling out onto the road.

In the ten years Jace has been my partner, I've consistently heard about drama with his dad, and I can't imagine what that's like. Mine is the best, and he does nothing but endlessly support Brody and me.

"Sorry, man. It's a tough spot to be in, I'm sure."

"My dad has always been hard on us, but damn, Drew can never get a break with him. Drew didn't even want the business, but he also didn't want it to get taken over by some random person with the right check amount. So he busted his ass to keep it in the family, to get where he is, and Dad just can't let him do it. I don't want to see it come between them, and Mom has reached the end of her rope."

"Wish I had some advice for you, but I got nothing."

"Don't worry about it." Jace waves his hand at me as he drives, the morning bright and clear. Traffic is minimal for once, and people seem to be on their best behavior. For now at least.

"How are you and Sadie doing?" Jace asks. Stopping at a red light, he grabs his coffee and takes a sip, looking over at me.

"We're good. She's starting to look into business ventures. She wants to get away from the bar, and I don't blame her. She's switched back to earlier shifts."

"Good for her."

"I'm really proud of her. That girl of mine, she's something all right."

"Yeah, she's stuck with you. That poor, poor thing."

I smack his arm, and Jace laughs. The light turns green, the car moving once more.

We've only been driving in silence for a few minutes when we get our first call. Jace flips the sirens and we take off, our job never quiet for long.

§

"Honey, I'm home," Sadie jokes, and I turn from the stove where I'm cooking dinner. I got off work about an hour ago, while she stayed later to help Brody out since the closing waitress came in late.

"Hi. Damn, am I glad you're home." Setting the spatula down, I rush over to scoop her into my arms.

"Everything okay?" she asks, and I shake my head. "Garret?"

"Long day," I tell her, and she runs her fingers through my hair.

Pulling away from her, I give her a gentle kiss and then turn back to finish dinner.

"What are you making?" she inquires, wrapping her arms around my waist from behind.

"Spaghetti. One of the few things I don't burn. Sound okay to you?"

"Yeah, sounds good. So I was thinking… this weekend, could we do something?"

"Yeah, sure babe. What did you have in mind?" Turning the burner to simmer, I sit with her at the dining table.

"Well, I was thinking—and you can tell me no if you don't want to, plus I have no idea how far it is—but I wanted to see Pigeon Forge and Gatlinburg."

"You haven't been there yet?"

"No, and I've been reading about it. I really want to go."

"How about we do something even cooler?" I ask, and she smiles.

"Like what?"

"What if we go to Dollywood instead?"

"What's that?"

My eyes go wide and my jaw drops. "You don't know what it is? Babe, it's the Dolly Parton theme park."

"Just messing with you, Walker. Hell yeah, let's go. But only if you wear a cowboy hat."

I laugh and stand from the table to finish dinner. "I don't have one, but you know I could rock the shit out of it."

"Damn right you would. Your baseball hat will do just fine though."

"Well good, because that's what I planned on wearing. Now, if your sassy mouth is finished, dinner is done. Shall we eat?"

"Yeah, I suppose so. You slaved for hours making this for us."

Sadie is awfully feisty tonight, and her plus me plus a bed is definitely happening the second she's done eating. I love it when she's like this, and all it does is make my dick hard.

§

An hour later, I'm in bed with Sadie, that sinful fucking mouth wrapped around my cock. After we tumbled into bed, I made her come twice on my tongue before she flipped us over and took advantage. My eyes are heavy-lidded, and she looks up at me, nothing but lust on her face.

"Fuck," I grunt, thrusting gently. Her nails scrape down my thighs and I shiver. She's killing me here. "Baby, you gotta stop. I'm way too close."

She shakes her head and keeps going, one hand twisting around the base. My eyes shut and I fall back onto the bed, completely at her mercy. "Shit. Fuck, Sades. C'mon, I'm so—"

She takes me deep into her throat and swallows, and that's all I can take. My back arches and sweat breaks out on my skin as I come, my body shuddering through an intense-as-hell orgasm.

She releases me with a wet pop and rises to her knees. "Good?"

"Dumb thing to ask a man who's barely conscious from that."

"Glad you enjoyed it." Sadie crawls up the bed and lies down next to me, throwing her arm across my chest.

"Give me ten minutes. Then that pussy is fucking mine."

Her cheeks redden, and I'm pretty sure it's the lust that's still running through her. Tucking her into my side,

I trail my fingers up and down her bare back, scratching lightly.

Ten minutes later, I make good on that promise.

Twice.

CHAPTER TWENTY-ONE

SADIE

Dollywood was everything magical and more. We had so much fun, and Garret even got me on a few rides. We watched a jamboree show, and he slow danced with me.

Magical, I'm tellin' ya.

And Garret? That man is something all right. I told him months ago that he was like a book boyfriend come to life, and I wasn't lying. He really is. I didn't think men like him existed, and every day, he gives me something new to fall in love with.

Mitchell called me this morning and let me know that everything was going well, and that it wouldn't be much longer till I was a free woman. I'm happier than I've ever been, and I don't want anything to ruin it.

Wiping the table down with a rag, I look up when Lindsey shouts my name. She's standing in front of the bar with her arms full of plates. I drop the rag and hurry over to help her, taking a few plates from her.

"Thanks, girl." We carry them all out back to the kitchen, and she leans back on the counter. "I'm telling you, Brody needs to hire some new employees. I'm beat."

"How's the hospital?" I ask, setting the plates in the sink.

"It's good. They're having to remodel a wing of the ER, so my shifts have been cut in half. It's why I've been here so much this summer and fall, but I'm exhausted. I need to stick to one job, because my ass is done with this."

Laughing, I gesture at the apron I'm wearing. "You're preaching to the choir, Linds. I'm almost thirty. I need to start looking into saving some damn money and start putting my degree to use. It's time, I think."

"What do you want to do?" she asks. We stroll back out to the bar, the silence of a closing shift so much different than when the bar is hustling all evening.

"Well, when I got my degree, I wanted to open a trendy clothing shop, but it's not what I really want anymore. I've been thinking about it a lot lately, and I know what I'm gonna do."

"Drum roll, please," Lindsey jokes, and we both start laughing.

"I want to open a kid's store. Clothes, toys, furniture. I think it would be really cool, and there aren't any shops like that unless you go into the city."

"Girl, that's an amazing idea!" Lindsey cheers, and I give her a hug.

"I haven't told Garret yet, but I really want to do this."

"And you should. He'll support you completely, but you already know that."

"Yeah, I do. We won the lottery with those Walker brothers."

I can see the love in her eyes, and I'm sure mine mirror it. We're the luckiest women in the world to have those men as our own.

Silently, we finish getting the tables cleaned and then I'm off, heading home. Because it's a weekday, the bar was only open until ten, and we were able to start cleaning early, so it's only twenty after.

I wish I was going to Garret's, but he agreed to work a night shift tonight, he and Jace needing the overtime.

When I pull into my driveway, I head inside and lock the door behind me. Slinging my purse onto the couch, I walk into my kitchen to grab a water. Stopping in my bedroom to change into a pair of leggings and one of Garret's PD shirts, I flip the television on to a rerun of *Supernatural* and get comfy on the couch. Halfway through, I head back into the kitchen to snag a piece of the cheesecake I bought at the store on Monday.

Settling back down, I check the clock on my phone and see it's almost eleven. I'm tired, but I want to wait a little longer so I can call Garret before bed. Hitting Play, I focus on the show once more. Dean Winchester is the hottest character on TV. And anyone who says otherwise is lying.

There's a pounding on my door a minute later, and I pause the show, pushing the blanket on my lap off to the side. Walking to the peephole, I look out but don't see anything. Undoing the locks, I pull the door open and still don't see anybody.

Then I look left.

"Well, what do you know? Hello, Sadie. Good to see you, darling wife."

Graham Ward stands on the side of my porch, arms crossed over his chest. He looks strangely calm, a sick smile on his face.

"What… what are you doing here? How did you—"

"How did I find you? You served me with papers, dumbass. It had your address on them."

My address? I thought they left that out? I knew I should have filed the restraining order first. Fuck.

"You need to leave, Graham. You and I have been done since I left. And you're violating the restraining order, I'm calling the cops." I turn to go back inside when he grabs my arm, twisting it behind my back and causing me to cry out in pain.

"You will not do that. You're going inside, you're packing your shit, and you're coming with me. You do not get to decide when we're over, I do, and your tantrum was sufficient. And when we get home, you're gonna fucking pay for what you've done. Got it?"

"No. I'm not the same person I was when I left you. And you're hurting me. Let go."

"Oh, sweetheart, you haven't even felt pain yet. Trust me." Graham is in my face, but when he's least expecting it, I bring my knee up and ram him in the balls. He releases my arm, which gives me just enough time to run inside and lock the door.

Tears running down my cheeks, I grab my phone from the couch and dial.

"911, what is your emergency?"

"My husband just showed up at my house. There's a restraining order on him, and I'm scared. Please, help me."

"Ma'am, it's going to be okay. Can I have your address, please?"

"42 Birch Falls Road."

"Okay, we've alerted authorities. Are you inside your home?"

"Yes. He was hurting me, so I kicked him and ran inside. My doors are locked."

The operator begins trying to soothe me, but the loud crash of my front door shaking on its hinges has me screaming.

"He's breaking the door down! Please, tell them to hurry."

"Ma'am, they're only a few minutes away. You're going to be okay."

The banging on my front door stops, and I'm standing alone in eerie silence.

"I think he's gone," I say to the operator. "I can't hear him anymore."

"Officers are only five minutes out. They'll be there shortly, ma'am."

"Thank you."

But my relief is short-lived. My back door smashes open, Graham standing there with a look of plain rage on his face.

"No!" I scream.

"Ma'am, what's going on?"

Graham is on me before I get a chance to react, and he punches me hard, my body dropping to the floor. A ringing fills my ears, and I taste blood.

"What do I have to do to show you who is in fucking charge?"

"Graham, no. Please."

"Shut the fuck up, Sadie." He takes another shot at my face, bright lights flashing across my vision. He grabs me by the throat and hauls me to my feet, the pain in my head intensifying.

"No."

I fight him with all my might, just needing to hang on until the cops get here. My phone is still connected to the emergency operator, stuffed in my back pocket when he came through the door. Graham spins us so my back is against the kitchen counter and he chokes me harder, my vision starting to dim. He thinks he has the upper hand, but my groping hand finds a glass. With every last ounce of my strength, I smash it over his head, his body dropping to the floor.

Stumbling to my bedroom, I slam the door shut and lock it, then shove the small dresser as close to the door as I can before dropping behind my bed. My whole face is throbbing, and tears are splashing down my cheeks.

The police aren't here. And I know Graham isn't dead.

He's going to get in here. He's going to finish this, and then Garret will find my dead body.

Garret. No.

With shaky and fumbling hands, I get my phone from my back pocket and see that not only did the call disconnect, but I have a dozen texts from Garret.

Garret: What's happened? We're on our way.

Garret: Are you okay?

Garret: Baby, please, this isn't funny. Answer me.

Garret: Sadie, please tell me you're okay.

Garret: Fuck, baby, I need to know you're okay.

Sobbing quietly, I force my fingers to type out a message, my heart breaking with each word I write. Hitting Send, I slump down against the bed, my body growing more tired. My head is fuzzy, and it's hard to stay awake.

Please, Garret. Please get here.

Sadie: I'm so sorry, Garret. He found me. I love you so much. Thank you for loving me.

CHAPTER TWENTY-TWO

GARRET

"Dude, hurry up. I'm starving."

Parked outside a fast food restaurant downtown, I wait patiently for Jace to hurry his ass up so we can go inside. He's on the phone with his brother, and at this point, I'm ready to go in without him.

I tap on the roof of the cruiser, checking my watch—10:50 p.m. We've been on shift since one, and we have about three hours left. I'm tired as shit, missing my girl, and ready to clock my partner in the head. I want a shitty burger and I want it now.

I go to yank the door open to yell at him when he finally climbs out of the car.

"We need to go. Now."

"Fuck."

Dropping back into the car, I buckle up and look over at Jace. "What do we got?"

"Domestic break-in." His face is white as a ghost as he tears out of the parking lot, lights and sirens blaring.

"What's the rush, man?"

Jace looks over at me, and I'm taken aback by the fear on his face.

"It's Sadie's place, bro. And the operator heard a commotion in the background, and screaming."

My heart drops and I rip my phone from my pocket, firing off texts to Sadie. She doesn't respond, and when I try calling her, there's no answer.

"Please tell me it's not Graham. Please!" I shout, slamming my fist against the door.

"Calm down, man. I need you to stay calm. We can't help her if you lose your head."

"Get us the fuck there. *Now*, Jace. Stop fucking talking to me like I'm a damn woman in labor. I'm not gonna calm down. Get me to her."

Jace flexes his fingers on the steering wheel and focuses on the road. I feel like a dick for speaking to him that way, but my anxiety level is through the roof. I have no idea what's happening, if she's okay, and I'm not gonna be able to breathe until we get there.

My phone chimes with a text and I check it instantly, my heart dropping.

Sadie: I'm so sorry, Garret. He found me. I love you so much. Thank you for loving me.

"No, goddamn it, don't you fucking say goodbye to me," I shout, tapping out a message and hoping she sees it.

Garret: No, baby. Don't you do that to me. We're

almost there.

On a normal drive, our ETA would've been fifteen minutes, but we make the drive in less than ten. Jace radioed for backup as soon as we got going, so there might be people there already, but I have no idea.

"Fuck, man, let her be okay," I mutter, and Jace reaches over to squeeze my shoulder.

"She will, Garret. Have faith. She's a tough one. She's okay. You need to keep it together."

"Fuck!" I roar, my teeth gritted together.

Jace doesn't talk the rest of the drive. When we race onto her street, I don't see any other cruisers. We're first on the scene.

Please, baby. Please be okay.

Jace parks and we leap out, guns drawn. The house is silent, and the front door is closed. Jace motions to the front and I go around back. As I make my way toward the back porch, I see light spilling out from the back of the house. The back door's been kicked in and is standing wide open. Keeping my gun out in front of me, I take the few steps needed to get onto the porch, sweeping the doorway and making sure the room is clear.

Stepping inside her kitchen, I find a mess, as well as a small pool of blood. My heart is pounding loudly in my ears, and I'm struggling, terrified of what I'm going to find. As I spin around to clear the living room, I hear a loud bang and turn toward it, the noise coming from her bedroom.

A second later, there's an even louder smash, and this time I hear a sound that will never leave my head for the rest of my life—a soul-shattering scream belonging to Sadie.

I rush down the hallway, making sure to shout loudly. "Nashville PD!"

Light is filtering out of Sadie's bedroom, that door knocked in as well, her small dresser blocking half the doorway. I cross the threshold and find Graham standing over her, my girl's body pinned to the bed. His hands are around her throat, and she's kicking and hitting at him, her body tiny beneath his frame.

And in that moment, I see red.

Fuck protocol.

Fuck my job.

Gun back in its holster, I shove the dresser out of the way and grab Graham by the back of his shirt. In one swift move, he's off Sadie and flat on his back on the floor, a look of confusion all over his face. I cock my fist back and drive it straight into his nose, the satisfying crunch not nearly enough.

"Fucking piece of shit. How's it feel now, cocksucker?" I growl, sickened when he just smirks at me. I punch him again, and this time he doesn't smirk.

All I can see are Sadie's bruises.

I hear her nightmares.

Her tears.

Her pain.

I lift my arm again when it's grabbed from behind,

and I turn to find Jace there.

"Let go," I grit out, but Jace shakes his head, pulling me back from the bastard.

"Dude. No. You got your shot. Now go take care of your girl. Backup is one minute out, and the last thing I need is to explain why you're now the one about to be arrested."

"Fine." Shaking out of Jace's grip, I get to my feet and wipe my hand across my mouth. "Get this piece of shit out of here."

Jace begins to read him his Miranda rights, and the sound of his handcuffs is all the signal I need. Rushing to the bed, I kneel over Sadie and gently cup her face, making sure to check for a pulse. Her face is bruised, and there are darkening marks around her neck.

My hands shake when I brush her hair off her face, my eyes stinging.

"Sadie, baby, it's me, Garret. Can you open your eyes?"

I run my thumb over her cheek, and her eyes slowly creak open. When they focus on me, she starts to cry, her entire body racked with her sobs.

"Thank you, Jesus," I mumble, dropping my forehead to hers. "We got the call over the radio, and I was so fucking scared, baby."

"I fought him," she whispers, voice hoarse and cracking.

I nod, a few tears slipping out and falling down my cheek. "I'm so proud of you, Sades. You did so damn good, and now it's over."

"I'm so tired, Garret."

"I know, but the ambulance is almost here. I need you to stay awake, baby. Hold my hand and squeeze it tight. Don't close your eyes. Stay right here with me."

"I promise," she says, her voice so quiet that I can't do anything but sit and hold her, praying the entire time that she's going to be okay. That she'll make it through this.

The wailing sirens are loud, and I know the ambulance is here. Moments later, the paramedics race inside, pushing me away from her so they can do their jobs.

Sadie is taken out on a stretcher and I stumble outside, Jace speaking with our sergeant in front of our squad car.

When I make it over to them, Clarke looks at me with concern. "Is she okay?"

"Yeah, I think she is. It all looked superficial to me, but they're taking her to the hospital to get her checked out. I would never ask this normally, but can I...?"

Sarge just waves a hand at me, knowing exactly what I was about to ask. "Give me your full statement and then you can take off. Have Miller drive you to the hospital. Now, let's go over what happened."

Crossing my arms over my chest, I give him the full play-by-play, not leaving out a single detail. Once we're finished, he tells me to come into the station in the morning and get everything written up. Jace and I climb into the cruiser a moment later, and he takes me over to Memorial. The drive is completely silent; I'm too drained to speak.

I'm so angry, and while I know Sadie's okay, right now

I'm the furthest thing from it. I'm about to splinter into a million pieces, and my emotions are absolutely fried. I need to see her and be with her right now. I'm angry that Jace didn't let me beat the ever-loving fuck out of him. I'm even angrier that he had the balls to come after her.

Graham Ward is a sick fucking bastard. He abused and degraded her for years, but then she finally gets away. Files for divorce and moves on, finds a new life for herself. She was healing, and then this filth comes after her, for what reason? Because he isn't in control anymore?

No, fuck that. I hope he gets his in prison, because with the violence tonight and the fact that he violated the restraining order, I'm sure he's facing hefty jail time. At least I hope he is.

I'm so lost in my mind that I barely notice Jace turning into the hospital parking lot. He pulls up to the emergency room entrance and stops the car at the curb. I go to jump out when he grabs my upper arm.

"Hold on a sec."

"What?" I ask, turning to look at him, still holding the door handle.

"I'm sorry, bro. I know you're angry I pulled you off Ward, but you gotta understand. Sadie was alive, and we both know just from how that place looked that she fought him something fucking strong. I couldn't let you risk your badge and your girl just to get your revenge. I let you hit him, but I knew those two wouldn't be enough for you."

"It's cool," I lie, and he smacks my arm.

"Garret, fucking stop, okay? You're a damn good cop. One of the best I know, and I also know how much you and Sadie love each other. You need to be out here, in the real world with her, not sitting behind bars because that fucker let you get the best of him. He's a scumbag, and you and I both know someone like him will get his ass kicked in jail. Be pissed at me all you want, but I did the right thing, and you know it."

I scrub a hand over my face and nod, knowing he's 100 percent correct. Jace isn't the enemy, and to be honest, deep down I'm glad he stopped me. I had no intention of ending my torrent of punches until that garbage was dead, and then where would I be?

"You're right. I'm sorry, I just can't think straight right now. I swear, Jace, when I saw him on top of her, I just lost it. I couldn't do anything but just take him the fuck down. I needed to make him feel the same pain Sadie felt. I wanted to fucking kill him."

"Me too, buddy," Jace says quietly, and he squeezes my shoulder. "Go see your girl. I'll be up in a bit. I just need to find a parking spot."

Without another word, I fly from the car, running into the ER. Since I'm still dressed in uniform, I don't even have to flash my badge to get back there, only stopping at the desk to ask where they took her. I'm directed to the farthest curtain on the end. Thanking the nurse, I rush toward it, ripping the curtain back to find Sadie sitting up on the hospital bed, drinking from a paper cup and straw.

"Baby," I breathe. Sitting down on the bed, I lean over

to kiss her cheek and reach for her hands, pulling them into mine.

"What took you so long?" she asks, voice still scratchy.

"Oh, you know. Had to drop Jace off at the strip club, and then I went to grab dinner, the usual."

Sadie bursts out laughing, and I do the same, cupping her face so I can press a kiss to her nose, then her lips.

"Are you okay?" I whisper, pulling back just a bit.

"I think so. Nothing's broken, and I don't have a concussion. I'm just sore."

"I'm glad, but that's not all I mean."

Biting down on her bottom lip, she shrugs, and I shake my head. "Babe, please don't shut me out. If you have something on your mind, just say it."

"I think there's something wrong with me," she whispers, and I raise an eyebrow.

"What?"

"I broke a glass against his head, Garret. And all I can think is, damn, now I have to clean broken shards of glass for the rest of my life."

Tossing my head back, I laugh loudly, looking back at her to see a small smile gracing her beautiful face.

"I'm okay, Garret. I can't let this ruin all my hard work. I may need some time with Dr. Klein to work through my emotions, but I promise not to hide from you. We'll do it together."

"I love you, Sades."

"I love you too. Thank you for saving me tonight."

"That's my job, baby. And it always will be."

Placing a gentle kiss to her forehead, I sink into the chair next to the bed and take her hand. Together, we sit in silence watching the late-night news.

I have no idea what tomorrow has in store for us, and I have no idea what Graham's arrest will bring, but one thing I do know is he's where he belongs, and Sadie is where she belongs.

By my side. Forever.

A knock on the doorway has us looking up, Jace standing there. He steps into the room and goes over to Sadie, bending down to kiss her cheek.

"You doing okay?" he asks, concern heavy in his tone.

Sadie nods at him and gives his hand a squeeze. "Yeah, I'll be all right. How was the strip club?"

"The what?"

Throwing my head back, I roar with laughter, Sadie joining in. Jace looks at the two of us like we have multiple heads, but we only laugh harder. Soon he just shakes his head and sinks into the other chair. We keep my girl company while we wait for the doctor to come back in, and I can't help sending up a prayer of thanks.

Tonight could've had a much more serious consequence, and I'm so grateful it didn't.

CHAPTER TWENTY-THREE

SADIE

Stepping out onto the back porch, I wrap my hands around the steaming mug of coffee and lean against the railing, the sun shining bright and the air cooler than it's been in a while. Enjoying the quiet morning, I close my eyes and reflect on the last couple weeks. Garret and I are in the best place we've ever been, and every day is better than the previous. He wants me to move in with him, but I'm not ready to let go of my little house. The kitchen is a space where I feel my mom more than anywhere, and in the early morning, when I'm having my tea or eating breakfast, I feel like she's with me. I don't want to lose that connection.

Garret has an interview next week for a detective position, and I just know he's gonna nail it. He's been a rock for me after Graham's attack, and I can never thank him enough. I stayed home from work for a week, and Garret took care of me every day, made dinner, held me when I had a nightmare, stayed up all night when I couldn't sleep.

I'm so in love with him that I can't even imagine a life without him.

He says he has a surprise for me this afternoon when he gets off work, so I'm just hanging around for the day. Carmen is gonna be here in a little while to visit, and to be honest, I need some time with my friend. She's the only person who understands me, who knows what I went through—not just a couple weeks ago but my entire time with Graham—and she's one of the best friends I've ever made.

Mom is gone, and the pain is there every day, but I've found my place here. I don't just have a boyfriend and friends. I have a family.

Finishing my coffee, I step back into my house and ignore the broken doorframe, placing the cup in the sink. Making my way to the bedroom, I change into a pair of jeans and a sweatshirt, one of Garret's he left here. Grabbing my latest Nora Roberts book, I shut the light off and go into the living room, curling up with it while I wait for Carmen to arrive.

Thirty pages later, I hear her car pull into the driveway. Closing the book, I go open the front door, Carmen flying up the steps and throwing her arms around me. I haven't seen her since that night, but we've talked every day. She knew I needed the space right after, but made sure I knew she was there for me as well.

Hugging her tight, I fight tears and she pulls back

to laugh, wiping her own away. "Sorry, I've just missed you. And when Garret gave everyone updates every day, I worried about you. Are you okay?"

Stepping inside, she tosses her purse onto the couch.

"Yeah, I am. Honestly. Graham is gone from my life, and he can't hurt me ever again. The first week was hard, but I'm feeling better every day. Garret helps with that."

"Hunter was the same way. It was hard with Craig, because I had to go through so many police interviews, mostly because of the attempted murder charges they nailed him with. But Hunt was there, strong and steady. He never broke, or if he did, I didn't see it."

"Garret broke a little," I tell her, my heart aching at the memory. "When we got home from the hospital, we went back to his house and he helped me take a shower. The bruises on my neck killed him, and that night he went down into the basement where his workout equipment is and took his anger out on the punching bag. Banged up his hands real good too. But then he came back upstairs and we moved past it."

"He loves you so much, babe. It's so damn obvious," Carmen tells me as we sit down on the couch together.

"I know. I love him that much too. I didn't think I would fall in love with him when I was still married and afraid all the time, but I did, and I'm not even sorry it happened that way."

"And you shouldn't be. Love doesn't work that way, and I think in some way we're all proof of that. Sometimes the heart just wants what the heart wants. And yours wanted Garret."

"Exactly."

Reaching for the remote, we decide to watch the latest Ryan Reynolds flick, and by the end I'm eager for Garret to come home. I miss him, even though it's only been hours since I last saw him.

And somewhere between a car chase and Ryan being flung from a car, I decide that maybe, just maybe, I'm ready to move in with him.

§

I'm pulling on an oversized sweater when Garret walks in my front door, wearing a pair of tight Wranglers and his black hoodie, a gray beanie pulled low on his head.

"Hey, you," he says, moving forward to give me a kiss. Releasing me, he steps aside so I can pull my boots on, then grab my light jacket. He gestures for me to go ahead, and I sling my purse over my shoulder, heading out the door. He locks it behind him and ushers me to his Jeep.

I have no idea what his surprise is, but he seems nervous and I place my hand on his leg while we're driving. "You okay?" I ask.

"Yeah, fine. I just hope you like it."

"It's from you, so I know I will."

Garret's smile is contagious as he drives us through downtown and toward the outskirts. He pulls his Jeep into the local cemetery, and I turn to look at him with my eyebrows raised.

What the hell are we doing here?

He parks at the end where there's open land behind all the headstones. Shutting off the vehicle, he turns to look at me with a serious expression.

"You ready?"

"I guess so. What are we doing here?"

"You'll see." Going around the hood of the Jeep, he meets me in the front and grabs my hand. "I love you, Sadie."

"I love you too."

With my hand tight in his, he walks us down the path, the afternoon still bright and sunny. Garret takes us down a row that looks like newer plots until we come to the end. Standing in front of me, he reaches down to cup my face and presses his forehead to mine. I band my arms around his waist and he pulls back to look down at me, his eyes shining and full of love.

"I know how much it hurts you that you never got to say goodbye to your mom. And I wanted to give you something that shows you how much I love you, and how much I would've loved your mom."

I tilt my head in question and he steps to the side, the headstone behind him coming into focus. In seconds my vision is blurry from tears.

Nacole Mary Parks

August 2ⁿᵈ 1965 – January 4ᵗʰ 2018

Beloved Mother

A butterfly is carved in the center, below the words,

and I can't keep it together anymore. Tears pour down my cheeks as I step forward, falling to my knees in front of it. I run my hands over the smooth stone and rest my forehead against it, sobbing harder than I ever have. Garret rest his hands on my shoulders, letting me have my moment. I finally pull away, wiping my cheeks with the backs of my hands.

"Garret."

"I know I should've asked you, but it never seemed the right way to start a conversation. I didn't know if you'd want to bury her ashes, and there was no way I could do that without asking. But this is where you can come when you need her. It gives you a place to visit, a place we can visit with our children one day, and you can tell them all about their nana."

My face falls and I stand up so I can hug him, burying my face in his sweatshirt. He cups the back of my head and I find the move comforting. I love this man so damn much, and I'm completely blown away that he did this for me.

"I love you," I tell him, pulling back so I can kiss him.

"I love you too, baby. And I hope this gives you some peace."

"It does. And the butterfly is perfect. I forgot I told you about that."

"I thought it looked nice."

"Thank you, Garret. Not just for this but everything. From the second you came into my life, you've made sure that I know I'm loved and taken care of. And I know I don't need to thank you, but I have to. I have no words for this," I say, running my hand over the stone again. My eyes are still teary, but it's a good teary. My mom got what she deserved, and I know without a doubt in my mind that she sent Garret to me.

I picked a random place in the entire country, and this man was here, just waiting for me. And I know I have my mother to thank for it. Missing her is something that will never go away, and the pain will always be strong. But I got Garret out of that pain, and for that, I can never be sad. I cherish everything about our life together, and I know the future will be filled with even more love and beauty than there is now.

"I'm gonna marry you, Sadie. I want to have lots of little babies, and I want them to be just as beautiful as their mommy. I want to get dogs and have lots of vacations and memories. I want to be sixty and still so fucking in love with you. I want everything, and I think this is just the beginning," Garret says, kissing my temple as we stand in the silence of the late afternoon.

"Even when I'm gray and tired and saggy?" I joke, and he laughs at me.

"Baby, I'm gonna love you forever, no matter what."

"I have no doubts." I smile, resting my head against his arm, and he moves it so he can pull me against his side. "And I'm ready to move in with you."

"Really?"

"Yeah. Part of my not wanting to was because it was my first real home after I left California. I bought it because the kitchen looked just like my mom's, and it felt like I had a piece of her with me. But now I have this special place to come to, and I don't need that house anymore. You're my home now, Garret. So it doesn't matter where I live, because with you, I'm always home."

"I love you so goddamn much," he says, and I just hug him tight. We're both feeling the emotions of this place, and I know Mom would've loved him too.

"Let's go home." I lean over to kiss the cool stone of Mom's headstone. "I love you," I whisper to her, and then hand in hand we walk back to his Jeep.

I'm pulling my seat belt on when a butterfly rests on the windshield. I smile through my tears and look over to see Garret smiling at me.

Taking my hand, he drives us home, and for the first time since I moved to Tennessee I feel the one thing I've wanted since I lost Mom.

Peace.

CHAPTER TWENTY-FOUR

GARRET

TWO MONTHS LATER

My boots crunch in the few inches of snow as I walk around my deck with a giant string of lights rolled into a ball, hanging them along the railing. Christmas is in just a couple of weeks, and I decided to go all out with decorations while Sadie is inside going through all the stuff we bought for the house. We got our Christmas tree this morning, setting it up in my living room in front of the large picture window. Then we went downtown to the little shop where they sell Christmas decorations and picked out the topper.

We made another trip to Target to get lights and even more stuff for the tree. She's been so excited and happy, but she has no idea what Christmas will bring her. I've had the small black box hidden in my nightstand for a little over a week, and I can't wait for Christmas Eve so I can give it to her. I had a custom ring made for her, and I know she's going to love it.

Using the staple gun, I attach the final section to the banister, stepping back to admire my work. The entire outline of our house is done up in lights, and I even made sure to do the entire outline of my garage too. I'm exhausted but it looks good. My dad will be proud.

Grabbing the staple gun, I carry it out to the garage and place it on my tool bench. Shutting the door, I stride back into the house, cold and needing coffee. Sadie's sitting cross-legged in the middle of the living room, looking through all the packages of bulbs, her short hair pulled into a ponytail. She reaches for the roll of ribbon she picked out and stands up.

"How's it looking out there?" she asks, coming to give me a kiss.

"Looks good. You'll have to wait till tonight to see if I really screwed it up though."

"Want some coffee? I was just gonna put on a pot."

"Yes, please." I kick my boots off at the door, hanging my coat on the hook.

As she fills the coffeepot with water, I notice she's not looking so good—bags under her eyes and her skin sort of pale.

"You feeling okay, babe?"

"Not really. I've been feeling crappy since we got home, and I'm tired. I want to get the tree trimmed though, and then I think I'm gonna take a nap."

"We can do that later if you want to go sleep now. We have all night to get it done."

She nods, her eyelids drooping. "I think I'm gonna do

that, just for an hour or so. Then we can do the tree, and I was thinking we could go out to dinner tonight."

"Sure. Go rest for a bit." Kissing her cheek, I take the canister of coffee from her. I hear her padding upstairs while I wait for the coffee to brew, so I pull the fridge open, taking out the glass dish with the apple pie in it. Sitting at the table, I grab a fork and just dig in, knowing she'll kill me when she sees I ate right from it.

Screw it. I just hung up seven billion lights and I'm hungry.

§

"I'm telling you, man. This is gonna be epic." Brody and I are hanging out in my parents' kitchen sharing a beer. They're holding their annual holiday party a week before Christmas, and we've ducked into the kitchen to grab drinks. He just told me they have a huge present for us tonight.

"Okay, bro. Whatever you say."

Sticking my free hand into my front pocket, I stride out to the living room where everybody is. I find my girl on the other side of the room, talking to Lindsey. She's in a dark green dress with black heels. She never dresses up, but we usually get fancy for this party. I'm in a red button-down and black slacks, and even my dad has on a tie.

Looking up from her glass of water, Sadie finds my eye and winks, her red lips turning up into a gigantic smile. I wink back at her and then go around the room to find my grandparents. Memaw and Papaw are two of my favorite people in the world, and the second they arrived, they grabbed Sadie and didn't let her go. They were so happy to see I'd finally found someone to settle down with.

Sadie still isn't feeling well. Lindsey told me she had the flu just a couple weeks ago, so we're sure she passed it on. As long as it doesn't hit me, I'm happy. Work is always crazy around the holidays, and with my job interview tomorrow, I need to be at my best.

"So, Garret, tell me. When are you gonna ask that pretty thing to marry you?" Memaw asks.

I laugh, leaning over so I can speak in her ear. "Next week, Memaw. The ring is already wrapped and under our tree."

"That's my boy." She smiles and squishes my face so she can kiss my cheek. Papaw just holds a hand out to me and I shake it.

I'm so happy to see how perfectly Sadie fits into our family, and how loved she is. I've been worried that this first Christmas without her mom would be really hard on her, but she's been so strong.

She's cut back at work, focusing on finding her path in life. For so long, she had to be silent and hidden in the background, waiting on a man who didn't deserve to even breathe the same air as her. Now she's finding her place in the world, and she's shining while doing it. I don't care what she chooses to do, as long as I get to be by her side.

A loud clanging draws my attention, and I see Brody

standing on top of the coffee table, a glass and knife in his hand. Rising from the couch, I rush around the outside of the room to find Sadie. She's standing alone near my mom, and I steal her for a quick kiss.

"Having fun?" I ask her, and she grins.

"So much."

Slinging my arm over her shoulder, I turn us when Brody starts talking.

"So, I know Christmas is still a week away, but we have a very special present for my parents and older brother. Can y'all come over here for a sec?"

I look down at Sadie, but she just beams at me and I shrug. She takes my beer from me, and I walk over to where Brody and Linds stand in front of my parents. Lindsey looks emotional, and I turn to my parents.

"First you need to put these on," Lindsey tells us, handing each of us a blindfold. Brody has a huge shit-eating grin on his face, so I decide to just go along with whatever this is.

Blindfolds in place, we stand there waiting.

"You know, man, if you wanted to kill me, the least you could do is not have an audience for it," I joke, and the room erupts in laughter. Nobody answers me though, and I feel something being pulled over my head.

"Put your arms through and take off your blindfolds," Brody announces, and I realize he put a T-shirt over my head.

Yanking my arms through the holes, I reach up and pull off the blindfold. Brody stands in front of us with his arm around Lindsey, who has tears in her eyes, and then I find Sadie, who's also teary. My parents and I look at each other and the reaction is instantaneous.

Grandma.

Grandpa.

Uncle.

"Shut the fuck up!" I yell. Grabbing my little brother, I pull him into the tightest bear hug I can, slapping him hard on the back. "Fuck yes, bro. Congratulations! I'm so damn happy for you."

"Thanks, man. I told you. Epic."

"Epic is an understatement."

Mom is bawling, and Brody releases me to go hug her. Reaching for Lindsey, I pull her into a tight embrace and she laughs.

"Congrats, Mommy," I tell her, and she cries harder. "When are you due?"

"June 20th. We find out the sex in a couple months."

"I'm so happy for you two. You'll make one hell of a mom, Linds."

"Thank you, Garret. We're telling my parents tonight."

"They're gonna flip." Kissing her on the cheek, I move past them all to my girlfriend, who's wiping her eyes with a cocktail napkin.

"Hey, Uncle Garret," she says, and I lift her into my arms.

"Did you know?"

"Linds told me when we got here. I'm so happy for them."

"Me too. Brody is gonna be a dad. I still remember when he used to follow me everywhere, wanting to do everything I did, and now look at him. Fuck."

"Proud of him, huh?"

"I'm so fucking proud of him."

The rest of the evening is spent celebrating the new addition coming next year. I'm so stoked to be an uncle, and I'm even happier for my brother. Today is a real good fucking day for our family, and I get to do it all with my girl by my side.

§

Waking up, I find Sadie sound asleep curled up against my chest. Pressing a kiss to her forehead, I brush her hair off her face and coax her awake.

"Merry Christmas, baby," I whisper, and she moves so she can reach my lips for a kiss.

"Merry Christmas. Why are you up so early?" she mumbles, voice thick with sleep.

"I'm excited to see what Santa brought?" I joke.

She laughs, sitting up in bed. "Garret, it's like seven in the morning. Can't we sleep a little later?"

"No, now let's go!" Jumping off the bed, I pull on my plaid sleep pants and a long-sleeved henley. I can hear her grumbling behind me, and I hurry down the stairs so I can start a pot of coffee; my stomach is all nerves, and I need to get some caffeine in me before this happens.

Five minutes later, the coffee is brewing and Sadie

finally comes downstairs.

In matching pajama pants to mine and one of my department T-shirts, she looks beautiful. When I offer her coffee, she shakes her head, going for the teapot. Shrugging, I fill a mug with the delicious brew and turn to watch her.

"You feeling better, babe?"

"Yeah, for now anyway. I feel good."

She sets the teakettle on the stove to boil, and while we wait, she fills a plate with fruit and some toast, setting it on the counter. I reach for a grape and pop it into my mouth as Sadie grabs a mug from the cabinet. The water boils a minute later and she pours it in. Turning around, she blows on the steaming mug and I gesture to the living room.

"You ready for presents?"

"Yeah, let's do it."

She pads into the living room ahead of me, and damn right, I watch her ass go. No shame here—my woman is fucking beautiful, and I love everything about her. Setting her mug on the coffee table, she sits under the tree. There's a fairly decent stack under the tree, and she moves to the side so I can sit next to her.

"Garret, you didn't need to get me all of this," she chides, and I reach out to tuck her hair behind her ear.

"I didn't. A good portion of these are the gifts we'll be bringing to my parents' tonight for dinner."

"Oh, well that makes sense. Here, you open the first one."

Sadie hands me a large box and I take it, ripping the paper off. I open the gift box and find the leather jacket I mentioned wanting at the department store in Nashville. "Babe, you didn't."

She's sporting the biggest smile I've ever seen. "You're gonna look so handsome in it."

This girl.

Leaning over the box, I give her a passionate kiss. "Thank you. I love it."

"I only have one more gift for you, but that's the last one for you to open."

"Here, Sades. You open one." I hand her the box with the new Keurig machine I got her, and when she opens it, she whoops in delight. Twenty minutes later, there are only two presents under the tree, including the one I'm dying for her to open. I feel like I'm gonna puke all over the tree.

Handing her the box, I pat myself on the back for the clever wrapping. I asked the woman at the jewelry store to put the ring in the largest box she could find, so it wouldn't give it away. Sadie rips the paper off and tosses it to the side, the gray box large in her hands. She snaps the top up and her eyes widen in shock.

Moving to kneel in front of her, I take her left hand in mine and look into her eyes, tears already spilling down her cheeks.

"Sadie Nacole, from the second you came into my life, you've changed me in every way possible. My life wouldn't mean anything to me without you by my side. I love you so much. Will you marry me, baby?"

Through her tears, she nods, her brilliant smile spanning her face.

"Yes. Yes, Garret Walker, I will marry you."

Launching herself into my lap, she devours my mouth, arms wrapped around my shoulders as I hold her to me. When she breaks the kiss and pulls away, I take the box out of her hand and pluck the ring from it. Holding her shaking hand in mine, I slip the one-carat princess-cut diamond onto her finger, the ring sparkling against the Christmas tree lights.

She cups my face and kisses me again, her happiness radiating and my smile just as big.

"I love you so much," she whispers, and I press a kiss to her forehead.

"I love you too. Merry Christmas."

"There's still one more gift."

She sniffles and reaches under the tree, staying on my lap. The small package she hands me is light, and I shake it next to my ear, making her laugh.

Tearing the paper away, I find another gift box, which I pop open, sifting through the tissue paper until I reach a small piece of white cloth. Unfolding it, I realize it's a tiny little unitard-looking thing.

"Babe, that's not exactly my size," I tell her, and she turns it over in my hands.

Daddy's Little Officer.

I'm pretty sure my heart has stopped beating.

I look up at Sadie, my jaw dropped, and she starts

crying. "Are you…? Are we…?"

She reaches into the tree for an envelope, pulling it open to slide out a small photo that she hands to me.

It's an ultrasound picture.

"I'm pregnant," she tells me, and I shove everything away from me to lay her down on the floor, hovering over her while I kiss her until we're both breathless and I'm not sure whose tears are on our faces.

"I'm gonna be a dad?" I ask.

"Yeah. I'm due July 9th. I was eight weeks on Monday."

"But we've always used condoms," I say, trying to figure out how this happened.

"Yeah, I have no idea. I told my doctor that, and she said sometimes it can fail. I don't know how, but I'm pregnant."

"You just made me the happiest man in the entire world, babe. Now, can I ask you something else?"

"What?" She looks up at me through her long lashes.

"Is it safe to have sex during pregnancy?"

"Yeah, why?"

"Because I really need you upstairs in our bed. Like now."

"Can I ask you something, Garret?" She bites down on her bottom lip.

"What?"

"We don't need to use those condoms anymore, so why do we need to go upstairs?"

"You're gonna kill me, baby."

This Christmas is one I'll never forget. Not only did

the woman of my dreams agree to marry me, but she's also carrying our first child. I couldn't love her any more than I do at this exact moment.

Sadie always says she thinks her mom brought us together somehow, and I know she's right.

Sadie Ward was meant to be mine.

EPILOGUE

SADIE

"Come on, Sades. You can do it, baby. Push, push, push."

My head falls back onto my shoulders, my hair soaked in sweat and my body aching in every way possible. I'm sure I look terrible, and I don't even want to know how many random people have seen my vagina today. But I also don't care. Fourteen hours of labor will do that to a person, I suppose.

"Come on, Sadie. One more big push and you get to meet your baby." Dr. Reed smiles up at me and I jerk a nod, determined to do this. Garret has a hand on one of my legs, the other crushed in my grip, but he doesn't complain once.

"You can do this, baby."

"Okay, Sadie, I need you to push as hard as you can, okay? Here we go. One, two, push!"

Tucking my chin to my chest, I scream and push with

all my might. I swear it feels like I'm going to pass out, and then the most beautiful thing happens—I fall back against the bed and the high-pitched cries of our baby fill the room.

"It's a girl!" Dr. Reed exclaims, and I start to cry, Garret's head on my shoulder.

"You fucking did it, Sades. I love you so much."

"Would Daddy like to cut the cord?" Dr. Reed asks, and Garret nods, stepping forward immediately.

A tear runs down his cheek when he sees our little girl for the first time, and then she's placed on my chest, the most perfect little human alive. Gripping her tiny little fingers, I bring them to my lips and shift her around so I can see her sweet face.

"Hi, baby," I whisper. "We've been waiting to meet you for so long."

Garret sits on the bed next to me and lays his head on my shoulder, both of us staring down at her, her big eyes blinking open so she can gaze around the room.

"What do you want to name her?" he asks, and I look at him with tears in my eyes.

"I liked your name best," I tell him. We never found out the sex of the baby, so we each picked a boy name and a girl name. His girl name was secretly my favorite.

"Are you sure?" he asks and I nod, resting my cheek on her little head.

"Well then, happy birthday, Hadley Nacole Walker. Daddy loves you so much, sweetheart." He rubs his thumb over her forehead and her eyes close, her fingers wrapped completely around my finger.

"Thank you," Garret murmurs to me, turning his head to give me a soft kiss.

"For what?" I ask, forehead resting against his.

"For everything. And thank you, Nacole, for giving me my girls. We love you, Nana."

I cry softly, then start laughing when Hadley coos in her sleep.

Our daughter is perfect.

§

Hours later, Hadley is asleep in her little bassinet and I'm completely in love. After they cleaned us up, they changed the sheets on the bed and now I'm back resting, waiting for Garret to get in here with his family. They've all been waiting to meet Hadley, and I can't wait for them to see her. She looks just like Garret, and I'm hoping she has his blue eyes. They're my favorite feature of his, after all.

Garret and I got married one month after Christmas. We exchanged vows in front of our friends and his parents, Brody standing by his side as his best man. Carmen was my maid of honor, and they made sure my mom was included in the ceremony. It was short and sweet, and absolutely perfect.

The second I became Sadie Walker was the first day of the rest of my life. Now we have a beautiful little girl, and life is perfect.

A soft knock on the door has me looking up from my perfect bundle, Garret stepping into the room with our visitors behind him. Keith and Angela—or Granny and Poppa, as they're now known—step into the room with Brody and Lindsey right behind them, their one-month-old son, Paxton, in Lindsey's arms. I didn't think babies were allowed in unless they were siblings, but clearly Lindsey working at the hospital gave her the in.

"Sorry, Pax wanted to meet his new baby cousin." She smiles, and I reach out to give her a hug. "She's so beautiful. Congratulations."

"All right, Uncle Brody needs to get in on this love fest," Brody jokes, and I hand him his niece. He tucks her into his arms and rocks her back and forth.

"Hey there, sweet girl. I'm your Uncle Brody, and we're gonna get in so much trouble together. See, your daddy is my big brother, and trouble is in our blood."

Garret laughs and rests his hands on his hips. His platinum wedding band shines in the fluorescent lighting, and my heart swells with pride for my new husband. My new detective husband, that is. Garret got the call three days after Christmas with the job offer, and I couldn't be prouder of him.

Brody passes Hadley off to her granny, and my mother in-law starts gushing about how beautiful she is.

Sitting in my hospital room, I look around at the most important people in my life, and I feel so damn blessed to have them. I'm one lucky girl, and now I know my daughter is the luckiest.

I'm telling you, life sure works in mysterious ways.

§

GARRET

Sitting in the dark nursery, I sway Hadley back and forth in the rocking chair, softly humming to help her fall asleep. She's the sweetest little thing, and it's crazy how such a small little girl could bring me to my knees. She takes my breath away, just like my beautiful wife. My girls are my life, and every day I show them just how much I love them.

A few minutes later, I carefully set Hadley in her crib and kiss her tiny cheek, her impossibly small hands curled up next to her face. Tiptoeing out of the room, I leave the door open a crack and walk down the hall to our bedroom. Sadie's asleep in the middle of the bed, completely wiped out. Hadley is three weeks old, and time is already flying by.

Pulling the blankets back, I climb into bed with my wife and fold myself around her. She wakes up and turns back to look at me. "Is she asleep?"

"Yeah, went back down easily. How are you doing,

Momma?"

"Tired. I didn't mean to fall asleep again. I wanted to go get something to eat. Did you want anything?" Sitting up in bed, she climbs out and slides her feet into her slippers.

"No, I'm good, but I'll come with you."

I grab the baby monitor from my nightstand, and we slip downstairs and head to the kitchen. I help her take a seat on one of the stools around the island, then open the fridge.

"What do you want, baby?"

"I was just gonna make a grilled cheese or something."

"Grilled cheese, coming right up."

Bending down, I grab the pan and place it on the burner. Ten minutes later, I slide her sandwich onto a plate and hand it to her.

"Thank you," she says, taking a bite, groaning in delight.

"Glad you like it, Sades, but if you could not make noises like that when I can't make love to you, that'd be great."

Sadie laughs around a mouthful of food, and I smirk at her.

"My bad," she mumbles, and I roll my eyes.

"You aren't sorry."

"Nope."

Grabbing a water from the fridge, I hand it to her and open one for myself. She's only just finished her sandwich when Hadley starts crying, both of us laughing at how even though she's upset, she still sounds so damn cute. Sadie tells me she'll grab her, and I stay behind to clean up the plate and other dishes.

Switching off the kitchen light, I head upstairs. Sadie's in the middle of our bed, breastfeeding our girl. Sitting next to her, I switch the television on and find some reruns of *Criminal Minds,* turning the volume down to a low rumble and pulling the blankets up to my waist. The soft glow of the TV washes over Sadie's face, and I turn to look at her, finding her smiling right at me.

"What?" I ask, leaning forward to run my fingers up and down Hadley's arm.

"I want at least two more babies," she says.

I laugh, resting my chin on her shoulder so I can look down at our daughter. "I'm good with that, babe."

"We have such a beautiful life, and I'm so grateful for you. You work so hard for us, and I'm so proud of you."

My throat swells with emotion at her words. Taking her lips in a soft kiss, I look back down at Hadley.

"I love our life, and I'm grateful for you too, sweetheart. Every morning I wake up and think, 'How the fuck did I get so lucky?' Your mom would be so proud of you too, and I know she's looking down on you every day."

"Me too."

Hadley finishes eating soon after, and Sadie doesn't put her back in her room, setting her in the tiny bassinet we have in our room instead and then climbing back into bed with me. With the two pieces of my heart in the room with me, I switch off the end table light and roll over so

I'm lying face-to-face with Sadie.

"I love you, Garret."

"Love you too, Sadie. Get some sleep. I'll be here all night if you need me."

Resting her face in the crook of my neck, she falls asleep and I follow not long after her, my sleep peaceful with no dreams to wake me up.

After all, why do I need to dream when everything I need in life is right next to me?

I already have my dream.

Forever.

The End

ACKNOWLEDGEMENTS

My husband: Thank you for being my rock. Always. I love you.

Heather, Nancy, Janell: If only you knew how much you meant to me, and this journey. I love you so much. Thank you for being my constants. And no, I'll never stop bringing the evil, you love it. You know you do.

Marcie: I would, without a doubt, be lost without you. I love you more than anything.

Heather & My Mady: I love you. So much more than you know.

Stacey: My boo. My favorite person ever. Thank you for everything you do. #LeoPapi

Kathy, Leaona, Heidi: Thank you for being my crew. I want to be you when I grow up. Love you.

Renee, Teri: My beautiful ladies. I love you. So glad I found you two.

Lisa: I love everything about our friendship. I'm so grateful this book world brought us together and I love you.

Kristin: You really are the best editor a girl could ask for. I adore you, and one day I will use that word in my book. Promise.

Melissa: Slaying my covers since the beginning and I love your crazy talented self.

Juliana: Thank you for the amazing work. Best formatter ever!

Golden: We finally got Furious together! You inspire me every day in all walks of life and I'm so grateful to have finally collaborated. I see many more in our future.

Robert: You've been nothing but a constant support system, friend, and colleague. I am so honored to have this cover with you, and everything about Garret Walker is embodied in your kind and genuine soul. I wish you nothing but continued success and I know that you'll change this world one day.

Lydia: I am so glad that I chose to work with HEA and I am so grateful for all the hard work. You're absolutely amazing!

My Lovelies: Without you I'm nothing. And I mean that in every way. I love you all.

My readers: Thank you, times a million, times infinity. I love you.

ABOUT THE AUTHOR

Born and raised in New England, Heather Lyn lives in Southern Maine with her husband and son. When she doesn't have her nose in a book, you can generally find her listening to country music or drinking coffee. Proficient in sarcasm, she enjoys bringing as much life to her books as she can. With a lifelong love of reading and storytelling, she decided to try her hand at self-publishing in 2016, when she released her debut novel.

Follow Heather on Facebook

facebook.com/authorheatherlyn

Made in the USA
Middletown, DE
06 January 2019